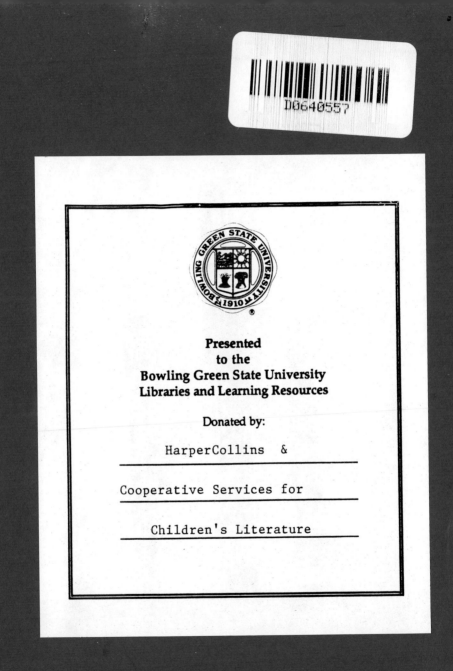

ACTING NORMAL

NORMAL

Julia Hoban

HarperCollins*Publishers*

Library of Congress Cataloging-in-Publication Data
Hoban, Julia.
    Acting normal / Julia Hoban.
      p.   cm.
    Summary: Having had a nervous breakdown brought on by repressed memories
unearthed in her acting class, eighteen-year-old Stephanie tries to recover and resume
a normal life.
    ISBN 0-06-023519-5
    [1. Emotional problems—Fiction.   2. Acting—Fiction.   3. Child abuse—Fiction.]
I. Title.
PZ7.H63487Ac   1998   97-49660
[Fic]–dc21   CIP
                                                                    AC

Typography by Christine Kettner
1   2   3   4   5   6   7   8   9   10
❖
First Edition
Visit us on the World Wide Web!
http://www.harperchildrens.com

For my mother . . .
and for my Henry

CHAPTER ONE

"Hey, could you tell me where I go to register?"

"Are you a new student or returning?"

"New." Raw, as a matter of fact, but he didn't have to know that.

"Go down the hall, turn left, room 212."

His directions were easy enough, but that didn't stop the queasy feeling in my stomach. I hate school, and a new school where I didn't know anybody was even worse. Especially since I hadn't been in school for almost a year. Maybe it was better this way, though. After all, the kids at my old school would have wondered what had happened to me. I couldn't have taken all the stares, and the whispers behind my back. I'm sure some people would have asked me straight out why I'd left. They probably would think they were being cool by being so open. No, a new school was definitely better.

Why were the halls so long? So far paranoia was one of the few problems I'd been spared, but I was sure that the guys wandering around must have been staring at how fat my thighs are.

"Hey, Stephanie!" a girl yelled. I turned around. Who could possibly know me here? But the girl looked right through me and grabbed hold of a tall, skinny girl. They giggled wildly and hugged each other. I felt like a fool for turning.

Room 212 was crowded with tons of students. It looked like a casting call, all those anxious faces holding their pictures and résumés, hoping they'd be chosen. Only the kids here weren't actors any more than I was at that point, and they were just holding plain ordinary notebooks.

Some older students were sitting behind tables with files full of index cards. They looked like they were probably seniors. I was supposed to be a senior too.

"I hate lines, but at least if we're doing this we can't be studying," said the girl next to me.

"That's true, but I wish this didn't take so long." I turned to look at her. She was wearing what seemed like the standard uniform: sweatshirt, jeans, and boots. I was dressed pretty much the same way, and I was glad. At least I wouldn't stand out. I'd never worn clothes like that to school before, though, and it had been something of a struggle figuring out what to wear. In my other life, I used to go to school pretty decked out. Usually I had an audition to go to at the end of the day, with no time to change. Even if the audition was for something non-fancy like McDonald's, I'd still be in full on-camera makeup. Now my face was naked. It matched the way the rest of me felt. My hair was looking pretty different too. I used to have to wake up half an hour early to get it done on audition days. But the past year I barely had enough energy to wash it. I was wearing it in a ponytail, and looking around I could see that was pretty standard too.

"What's your name?" I asked the girl. I didn't really care, but I'd sort of made myself a halfhearted promise that I would try and talk to somebody for at least five minutes every day. I could feel sweat starting to trickle down my back, and my stomach wasn't that happy either. I decided that maybe five minutes every other week would be a good place to start.

"Karen. What's yours?"

"Stephanie. What grade are you in?"

"I'm a sophomore. You?"

"Sen—junior," I stuttered, but she didn't seem to notice.

"It's too bad you can't buy any coffee around here. I'm really tired. I overslept. Thank God I live only a block away."

"You're kidding! I live on East Seventy-seventh Street. It takes forever to get here."

"East Seventy-seventh Street! Wow, that's really a trek. Don't most of the kids in your neighborhood go to fancy prep schools? What are you doing down here?"

"Well, I . . ."

"Next."

It was my turn. I was glad I didn't have to answer her, because I wouldn't have known quite what to say. Something like, "Well, yeah, most of the kids in my neighborhood do go to private schools, and I did too, but you see, I've had a kind of unusual life. I used to be in TV commercials, but after a while it got to be too much, and I fell apart, and well . . ." She would have thought I was some kind of freak. I had to learn to act normal around these kids. Wasn't that the whole point of me being in a school like this, anyway? To hang around with normal kids? To see if some of it could rub off on me? It had taken me more time to figure out my stupid outfit for the first day of school than it ever had for any audition. But in a way this was more important. It was my return to the real world after the past year of never-never land.

When my last shrink had suggested that maybe I would be ready to go back to school in the fall, I'd said yes. I was so tired of being out of it that I figured any-thing had to be better than staying home and watching the paint dry. Of course Dr. Stevenson had a different expression for it—she accused me of contemplating my own navel. Needless to say, we didn't always see eye-to-eye about everything. Stevenson had insisted that a public school would be best for me. My parents had balked at that; they'd wanted me to go to Spence or Brearly. At least everyone agreed that it would have been impossible to return to my old school. Not after what had happened. But Dr. Stevenson was adamant. She kept insisting that I'd spent too much time in rarefied atmospheres, kind of like a hothouse flower. Going back to school had sounded like a pretty good idea at the time. Now, however, I wasn't so sure. The few sentences I'd exchanged with Karen or what-ever her name was already had me gasping for air.

"Miss?"

"Huh?"

"Miss?"

The kid behind the desk looked at me impatiently. He must have been asking my name for the past five minutes. It was on the tip of my tongue to say "fit" in answer to his "miss." After all, it was the way I felt, but . . .

"Holt. Stephanie Holt."

"I don't see you here," he said as he flipped through the index cards. He leaned over to the guy next to him.

"Hey, Paul, you got a Stephanie Holt?" He looked back at me.

"What are you, a junior or a senior?" he asked.

"Wait a second," the guy named Paul said. "I've got a note about you here. You're the kid who's staying back, right?"

Right, you creep. A couple of kids looked at me, and I began to blush.

Stop it, Stephanie, I told myself. *Nobody's interested in you. Stop being so embarrassed.* I tried to dredge up whatever acting ability I had left to cover what I was feeling. I was more than a little wary of going too deep, but it wasn't much of a reach to remember a really stupid bathroom-freshener commercial I'd done about two years ago. You know the kind. The ones where you've got a family smiling really inanely about how happy they are to have found a way to cover up the smell of shit. It was perfect for the way I was feeling right now. I looked at Paul with a positively regal smile, as appropriate to the way I was feeling as it had been when I filmed the commercial.

"You've got to go up and see the principal. Up the stairs—room 414."

By now the halls were empty. It was so huge compared to my last school. I had no idea how I'd find my way around. I had to walk up the stairs to room 414. My last school had an elevator. Oh well, stairs are better for your thighs. I suppose it made more sense this way, instead of taking an elevator all day and then going to the gym to use the StairMaster. Gym workouts were another thing that had fallen by the wayside when I entered never-never land. I think that was the reason my agent dropped me, as much as anything else. The fifteen pounds I'd put on had made it pretty hard to cast me.

I arrived on the fourth floor slightly out of breath. Maybe I'd been smoking cigarettes in my sleep. I didn't really think so, but anything was possible with me these days. All I knew was that a year ago I could have done an hour and a half on the stair machine without being winded. The door was open. I stepped in and tried to clear my throat to get the receptionist's attention. "Hi, I'm supposed to see the principal. My name's Stephanie Holt." The receptionist started leafing through an enormous appointment book, when all three of the phones on her desk lit up. "Go on in, Ms. Martin's free." She waved her hand toward an inner office. "I'm the only one out here today, and things are a little crazy with registration." She picked up two of the phones at once.

Ms. Martin's door was open, and I stood at the entrance for a second, unsure of what to do. She was signing some papers and didn't notice me. I knocked on the door frame.

"Yes?" she said, looking up. Gray hair in a bun, glasses. She looked like the head nurse at the hospital, but I pushed that thought out of my head as quickly as I could. That was the last thing that I wanted to think about. I'd read Dante's "Inferno" right before leaving school. He'd talked about hell having nine circles. I've got some news for Dante, he'd never been to the ridiculously named Pleasantville Hospice. I'm sure if he had, he would've placed it on about the fortieth rung.

"Hi, I'm Stephanie Holt. I'm supposed to talk to you instead of registering. My parents talked to you. . . ."

"Stephanie, of course, sit down. Your advisor and I have already worked out a schedule for you. If you have any problems with it, feel free to come and talk to us, but we'd like you to try it for at least two weeks. Okay?"

"Sure," I mumbled. I wondered what they'd fixed up for me.

"Here it is. As I told your parents, the fact that you

didn't leave school until after Christmas means that you do have almost half the credits you should for a senior, so last year won't be a total loss. Now, don't get too anxious about credits and things. If you feel comfortable, and it isn't too much pressure, you should be able to graduate next January, which is only half a year late. But you were always a year ahead anyway, weren't you?"

I nodded.

"So this should make you come out just about even. We're putting you in junior English and biology. You'll be in French four, along with the rest of the seniors, and precalculus, which is also a senior class. Your parents and I talked about the sessions with your psychiatrist not conflicting." I winced. "Monday, Wednesday, and Friday your English class ends at three-fifteen; that should leave you plenty of time to get to your four o'clock appointment. Tuesday and Thursday you'll have a study hall until four o'clock and finish the day along with everyone else. Make sense?"

"Sure. What do I call myself? A junior or a senior?"

"You're a little bit of both right now. Don't worry about that, though. And remember, any problems, just knock. But give it a couple of weeks."

"Thank you," I said, and stood up. I wondered whether I should shake her hand, but she was already busy with other papers on her desk. I took my schedule and left. As I got to the door, she called me back.

"Oh, Stephanie?"

I turned.

"By the way, if you're on any medication, you need to tell the school nurse." She smiled pleasantly.

"No, no medication." Not anymore, anyway.

I looked down at my schedule. Today was kind of a crazy day, what with registration and all; morning classes had been preempted by practical nonsense, and now it was almost the end of the day. That meant it was already time for English—junior English—on the third floor. I hoped it would be pretty easy, but enough to keep my mind off other things.

There were about thirty-five students in the class. I found an empty seat in the back of the room. Thank God. The last thing I wanted to do was be under the teacher's nose. I wondered if any of the teachers had been warned about me. If they had, I wondered what they had been told. I used to sit in the front row of my English class in my old school. The teacher figured that anyone who sat there wasn't afraid of being called on, so they must have done their homework. Of course, anyone with half a brain figured out the system right away. It wasn't that I didn't like school enough to do the work, but just try studying acting, trying to make it in commercials, and doing homework too. Anyway, the back row for me this year.

Everybody was screaming and yelling. I was so used to quiet, and to being by myself, that any kind of conversation sounded loud. They all seemed to know each other, and I felt like an outsider, as usual. I must have been the only new kid in the class. Then I noticed that the girl next to me wasn't talking to anyone. She had her notebook open and was drawing corny hearts and flowers around the name Daryll.

"What are you looking at, sweetheart? Don't you have anything of your own to read, or don't you know how?"

Huh? Why was she being so nasty? I hadn't done anything. Well, maybe I was being a little nosy, but still . . .

"Sorry," I said, looking her in the eye. She shrugged and went back to doodling. Even though I'd decided after my talk with Karen to hold off on trying to win the Ms. Congeniality contest, I felt self-conscious being the only other kid in the room who wasn't talking to someone. I could have tried my neighbor, but she didn't exactly seem too friendly. I just sat there and tried to look like I was perfectly happy being left out.

In a way, I was. I've never been very social, but—

"What's your name?"

I looked up, surprised. So she was going to talk to me after all.

"Stephanie."

"I'm Dahlia."

"Are you new?"

"New to this place, for sure. I don't look like the type to hang around here, do I?"

"What type hangs around here?"

"Dopes."

"You mean they take a lot of drugs?" I was surprised. I didn't think that my parents would have let me go to a school where that was a problem. They'd be worried sick that I'd add addiction to my repertoire of illnesses. I don't know why; I barely even took the drugs that they'd prescribed for me at Pleasantville.

Dahlia gave me a long stare. Did she recognize me? After all, I had done a fair number of commercials, so it wasn't completely inconceivable. Even though it would lead to a lot of awkward questions, it would make me feel special again too. I needed to feel that way again.

"You're new too, huh?" she said finally, breaking into a grin.

"Yeah, how could you tell?" I was a little bit

disappointed that she hadn't asked me if I was the girl in the Dannon commercial, which was still running. But I guess I wasn't that surprised. What with the weight, the different hair and clothes, and the lack of makeup, nobody would have believed that I'd once been on TV, let alone recognize me out of context. Still, I found myself smiling back at her. I was shocked at myself, until I realized that she was the first person to smile at me in the past year. Oh, people had certainly smiled at me, but in a nasty, patronizing way. She was smiling *with* me. "Listen, you don't really mean the kids here take drugs, do you?" I knew that she didn't mean that. I could tell from her smile that when she said *dopes* she meant *idiots*. I wondered if the fact that she could tell that I didn't fit in was a point of favor in her eyes. If that was true, she'd be the first person to ever think that way about me, and I wanted to keep talking to her.

"Nah. The only drugs around here are the pushers near Stuyvesant Park. I just meant they're not sophisticated. Like, my boyfriend is twenty-seven. He's in the Marines. He wouldn't go out with anyone around here." She looked at me appraisingly. "You got a boyfriend?"

I shifted in my seat.

"No."

"Yeah? How come? You're cute."

"Thanks." I looked at her; she was staring at me openly and didn't seem at all embarrassed by being so frank.

"So how come you don't have one?"

Maybe I had wanted to talk to her, but the conversation was starting to head in a bad direction, just like it had with Karen. I wasn't about to get into any kind of discussion about why I didn't have a boyfriend. Couldn't she just have kept talking about herself and her stupid Marine? "I just don't, that's all. Okay?"

"Oooo, touchy." But she smiled again, like she hadn't been offended. "Well, don't worry. You'll meet someone."

Just then the teacher came in, so everyone quieted down. Dahlia turned away from me and went back to drawing in her notebook.

"Hi, everyone, I'm Mr. Friedman," the teacher said. "This is an English lit class, as opposed to American lit, which you took as sophomores. There will be a quiz every two weeks, two written papers, and a final. I'm handing out photocopies of your reading list. We're going to be concentrating on short stories and novels. The stories are mostly nineteenth century. Hardy, Collins, et cetera. The novels are more contemporary.

We're going to start with *Rebecca* by Daphne du Maurier."

I looked around me. Dahlia was reading her horoscope in some magazine. A guy two seats in front of me was playing with a pocket Nintendo hidden from Mr. Friedman by his notebook. Two girls whispered to each other, and most of the other students just looked bored.

I was back in school.

CHAPTER TWO

Wednesday was my first session with my new psychiatrist. I hadn't really been to a psych for almost two months. My last shrink had tactfully let me know that she was getting rid of me at the end of July—"We just don't really have the kind of rapport necessary for any therapeutic work, Stephanie"—and there wasn't a shrink to be found during August. My parents had almost gone through the roof when Dr. Stevenson ended my therapy. I guess they thought that all they had to do was spend money on some fancy shrink and I'd be fine.

If you ask me, not having seen a shrink for two months hadn't done me any harm. I didn't think Dr. Stevenson or Dr. Marks before her had helped me much. At least they'd been a little better than the worthless guys at Pleasantville, but not by a lot. But maybe I only felt that way because I was nervous about seeing a new psych. To tell the truth, I was a little nervous about doing anything that would open up the whole can of worms, and God knows it would be mighty easy to let the whole mess come spilling out. Right there on the uptown bus. At a moment's notice I could be ready—I could feel my circle of attention narrowing, preparing me for that state which can't be unfamiliar to drug addicts but which good actors simply call concentration, and with that feeling came a surge of anger. How could I have let myself get to that point? Me, Stephanie. Wasn't I a girl who, if she hadn't been a child star, had at least been a long way from having to leave school because of "emotional problems"? But I wasn't that Stephanie anymore; now I was a girl who spent her time looking for a therapist with whom I could have a "rapport." I told myself that it was best not to think about this kind of stuff, to push it all down. Only my mind wouldn't obey, it wouldn't stop until it settled on one painful image and two disturbing words: *sense memory*.

My new psychiatrist's office wasn't exactly homey, but then again none of these places ever make you feel comfortable about spilling your guts out. In a way I found the sterility of it refreshing. It was a lot better than Dr. Stevenson's office, anyway. Hers had been decorated with a kind of forced homeyness, almost as if we were supposed to be friends, like I was just coming over for a cozy chat. But this looked like someplace where you could get work done. This place looked serious.

I was early, so I sat in the waiting room leafing through old magazines. After a few minutes I heard the front door close and a man poked his head around the corner.

"Stephanie? Hi, I'm Dr. Steinhart." He extended his hand. "Come on in and sit down."

"Sit down? Don't you mean lie down?"

"Sit down, lie down, whatever makes you feel most comfortable. As we get into therapy you'll probably feel better lying down. Right now I'd just like to get a few facts from you."

"Shoot."

"How old are you?"

"Eighteen."

"And because of your emotional breakdown you left school halfway through your junior year?"

He didn't mince words.

"Uh-huh. Anything else you want to know?"

"Does it make you uncomfortable to talk about your breakdown?"

I shrugged. No, darling, it's my favorite subject. But it would be okay as long as we didn't get into anything too deep, and with what was messing me up there'd be no chance it would occur to this guy on his own.

"Between last Christmas and today you've seen two therapists in private practice, and before that you were briefly hospitalized?"

"Uh-huh."

"And you had one-on-one psychiatric care at that facility as well?"

"Yeah, but I've never been to a man before, Dr. Steinhart."

"Most people call me Robert, or even Rob if they've had a big enough transference." He smiled at his joke. *Transference* is a term that pyschs like; it just means that you're getting along with them. "Anything you want to tell me about the hospital, any thoughts on why it didn't work out with the other two?"

"I didn't feel like talking to women shrinks, okay?"

"That's interesting. Usually people are more comfortable talking to someone of their own sex. Do you think that you'll feel more relaxed with me, then?"

He paused, as if he was expecting me to tell him that I thought everything was going to be just peachy between us. It was true that going to a man was a step in the right direction, and I had to admit that he already seemed a lot better than my other two shrinks, but things were still a million miles away from being relaxing.

"Stephanie?"

"Hmm?" I still didn't look at him. It's embarrassing to look at people when you're telling them stuff about yourself.

"How is your situation at home? Your parents seemed very concerned about you when they called to schedule. Would you say that you get along with them?"

Of course they'd seemed concerned, why wouldn't they? That was why they'd called him to begin with. If it was up to me I'd probably have gotten around to it by the fourth of never. Dr. Stevenson had always harped on the fact that I wouldn't get better until I started taking responsibility for things. I hoped that Dr. Steinhart—sorry, "Robert, or even Rob"—would be different. I looked over at him sitting in a leather chair with his legs crossed, and tried to get an idea of what kind of guy he was. He was kind of handsome, actually; whoever cast him as a shrink had done pretty well. I craned my neck to see if he had any elbow patches on his cashmere cardigan. Nope. Oh well, not everybody's into thorough characterizations. I was a little bit disappointed until I saw the row of pipes in the corner. A very effective touch. I wondered if they'd been his choice or the prop master's. I really had to stop thinking that my life was a movie and that everyone in it was an actor too. But it made it much easier to deal with stuff. I could sort of pretend nothing was real. The only problem was I'd been doing it for the past year, and it hadn't made things any better.

Good old Rob certainly had the shrink demeanor down well. I'd noticed that as a group they tended to use the same facial expressions. During the past year, whenever I'd been particularly bored in a session, I'd taken to classifying those expressions. There were about fifteen different ones in the standard repertoire. Maybe Rob would introduce me to some new ones, but right then he was doing what I think of as number five: compassionate concern without wanting to push. Number five seems to be a popular one, both Dr. Stevenson and Dr. Marks had usually started each session with it. It's a look that says they really want to know what's going on, but they're not going to force you. Of course, it could easily be replaced with number twelve: barely concealed exasperation. With Dr. Stevenson I always figured that if she hadn't been a shrink and I hadn't been her patient, she would have been all too happy to tell me where to stick my problems. Of course, I hadn't exactly made it easy for her. But Rob looked genuinely interested. Well, we were still new together, and it could wear off at any second, but he looked like he cared. He was probably wondering what I was doing in his office. After all, even though my parents had set up the appointment, they hadn't told him anything about me. They really weren't allowed to discuss anything like that with my shrinks—it's called confidentiality. It's even better than confession. I mean, what happened between these walls was completely private. Even if I told him I wanted to murder somebody, he wouldn't tell the cops. Not only was anything I said confidential, but he couldn't talk with anyone else about me either, unless it was one of my old shrinks or something. I knew my parents must have been bursting at the seams to let him in on all my dirty secrets, but that was their problem. For all this guy knew, I was there to talk about how unhappy I was that I didn't have enough money for a sex change operation. I wondered if I should do something like that. As far as he knew it would be the truth, and it was probably the closest I'd get to acting in the near future. . . .

"Stephanie?"

"Yeah?" Had I missed something?

"I asked how things were going at home. Any problems there?"

"Things are okay." Well, that was pretty much true, as far as it went. Even though we argued a lot, things never got really bloody, but they sure weren't the same anymore. Mostly we made polite chitchat. Or rather my parents did; I just grunted when I had enough energy to respond. That should have been enough to make them happy. When they'd visited me at Pleasantville I didn't even get it together enough to grunt. I knew it would take a long time for me to forget the way my mother had looked back then. I'd never seen her cry like that before. It still made me uncomfortable to think about it. There's something about your parents crying that just seems like one of those things you shouldn't see. I knew another thing too. The fact that I responded to my parents these days was hardly enough to make them jump for joy. We used to be pretty close. I'm an only child, and my mom and dad are pretty okay. We used to do stuff together. My mom loved going shopping to help me pick out clothes for auditions. And later, when I became interested in being a "serious" actress, she'd call my school sometimes on Wednesday afternoons and say my agent had just gotten me a booking. Then we'd go to a Broadway matinee together. My father could never make the matinees, but he used to love going to old movies with me on Sundays. I couldn't remember the last time that I had done any of those things with my parents, and I'm sure they missed that kind of stuff. Dr. Stevenson had suggested that the difference now was because of my anger. Anger at them, expressing itself as hostility. At least that's what she thought. As far as I was concerned, I had a reason to be angry with them, and besides, my parents had been acting strange ever since I got messed up. Especially my mother. I always felt like she was uncomfortable near me. My father's way of dealing with things was to act like he was a dad on a TV sitcom, like everything was perfect. Unlike my new shrink, however, he wasn't such great casting. For one thing, he always looked worried. And for another, unlike the fathers on TV shows, he shied away from touching me. I don't think he'd kissed me good-night once in the past year.

"Have you started school again?"

"A couple of days ago."

"And how was it?"

Well, that was certainly the topic of the week, in fact my last pseudo conversation with my parents had been about school.

"How's the new school?" my father had asked with an attempt at joviality. He'd definitely needed elbow patches on his sweater, and I should probably ask Rob if he could lend my father some of his pipes. There was no way my poor father could pull this act off without some heavy costume overhaul. Of course, if he really could have seemed cheerful it would have helped, but nobody's that good an actor.

"Fine," I mumbled.

"No, really, honey, do you think you can handle it?" my mother chimed in.

"What do you mean, 'handle it'? You mean if I can't I don't have to go? Do you mean handle it academically? I didn't lose my brains when I lost my mind, Mom. By the way, I wish you wouldn't look at me like that. If you keep frowning you're going to wrinkle, and you can't get collagen injections anymore—they've taken the stuff off the market," I snapped. At the time I'd thought that was a pretty clever answer. But I felt bad remembering the way my mother's face had crumpled. I'd wanted to get back at her for the way I thought she was treating me. I couldn't stand being patronized, but I think I hurt her more than I'd intended. Maybe Dr. Stevenson had been right.

"Stephanie?" Dr. Steinhart broke into my thoughts. "Can you tell me anything about how it felt to be back in school?"

How did it feel? That was a good question, actually, one I hadn't asked myself yet. I hadn't let myself think about it, just sort of floated along. Woke up, went to school, went home, did my homework if I felt like it, went to bed. A couple of times I had talked to Dahlia, but that was about it. Mostly it was just different.

I looked at the floor for a change.

"It's a lot different."

"Different from what? Your old school?"

"Very."

"And how is it different?"

"Well, for one thing it's totally new; I hardly know anybody there. At my last school most of the kids knew who I was. I mean, there weren't too many students around who were starring in TV commercials. That's one of the reasons my parents thought I should switch schools, so I could be anonymous and not have to deal with everyone asking me what had happened."

"Are you in touch with any of your old friends?"

What old friends? I felt like saying, but I didn't. I'd always been pretty much a loner. I just didn't fit in with that many people. I never had a "best friend," like other girls do. I wasn't an outcast or anything; I just went my own way. I used to hang around with Laurie once in a while, but I hadn't spoken to her in months. She was another commercial actress, but a different enough type for us usually not to feel too competitive with each other. We'd get together and go makeup shopping every so often. You wouldn't believe the amount of makeup you go through when you audition for commercials. Laurie had sent me a card a while ago, suggesting that we go check out the sales at MAC, this really hot makeup store in the Village. How could I even talk to someone like that after everything I'd been through? There'd been a girl at the hospital, Amy, who'd been really sweet in a sad, lost sort of way. In fact she would have been a perfect Ophelia. We'd promised to keep in touch after we got out, but I hadn't returned her call the one time that she'd phoned. I didn't really want to see anyone associated with that period in my life. That pretty much took care of the friends, or lack thereof, that I'd had from school, commercials, or my flirtation with organized medicine. As far as my "serious" acting friends went—they didn't. I'd never gotten along with anyone in my acting class. They were jealous of the fact that I made money in commercials, and even if that hadn't been the case, they were the last people on earth that I wanted to see now. I'd always wanted the kind of best friend that girls have in books and on TV. Now that I wasn't going to be an actress anymore, I'd have time for one too. It was too bad that I was so messed up. I mean, if I didn't feel comfortable with people before, it was nothing to the way I felt now. I just shrugged my shoulders and didn't say anything.

"Your parents mentioned that you were an actor," Dr. Steinhart continued. I guess he was fishing, trying to get me to respond to something. Poor Rob, I wasn't exactly being too forthcoming. I wondered if he'd switch to expression number twelve soon.

"Yeah, I was, I guess."

Hah! What would I have given, to be able to look anyone in the eye and really believe that I was an actor?

"You guess?"

"Yeah, well, I did a lot of TV commercials, but that's not really acting." Should I tell him about the rest of it? No, no way, not then. Maybe never.

"Do you still do commercials?"

I shook my head no.

"Because commercials aren't real acting?"

"Yes. No. I don't know. Even if I wanted to, I couldn't now because I don't have an agent anymore. She dropped me about a year ago when it became clear to everyone that I was out to lunch."

"That must have hurt."

"Hah! By then I'd been through stuff that made that look like a trip to the zoo." Oops, if I didn't watch it, I'd start giving away too much.

"What kind of stuff?"

He'd perked up right away on that one. Well, he could forget about it. "I'd rather talk about something else."

"You can talk about whatever you want; this is your time."

"Isn't it boring listening to people go on about themselves all day?" Dr. Stevenson had always acted as if it was.

"Boring?" Rob genuinely seemed confused. As if the suggestion was ludicrous.

"Yeah, my last shrink used to say I was too self-centered, that I talked about myself too much."

Rob smiled. "Stephanie, the point of being here is to talk about yourself. As for being self-centered, I don't know if that's a problem for you or not, but I will say one thing: I've yet to meet an eighteen-year-old who wasn't, or who didn't grow out of it. In any case, please don't worry about boring me; I'd be interested in whatever you have to say."

Well, that was somewhat encouraging, but unless I started carrying on about the sex change, I had nothing to talk about. We were both silent for a while.

"I'd like to hear a little more about your experience with commercials."

"Commercials are nothing. Really, don't be impressed with them. You don't need any talent to be able to do them. You've just got to have the right look, that's all." As I said that I wondered what he was thinking. I wasn't really happy about the weight I'd gained, or about any part of the way I looked. Maybe he didn't think that I looked good enough to be on TV.

Maybe I should bring him one of my head shots.

"Is that why you say they aren't real acting?"

"You got it. I always thought they were real too, but that was before . . ." I trailed off. After all this time, I should know to be more careful. But one thing leads to another when you're talking to psychs, and before you know it, they're getting pretty close to home.

"Before what?"

"Huh?"

"You started to say something."

Why not tell him? I mean, I certainly wasn't going to let him in on the whole story, but there was no harm in him hearing about this part, and it was a good memory, one of the few good ones. Besides, I felt like I owed him something for being nicer than Dr. Stevenson.

"Well, when I was fifteen I saw a movie . . ."

A movie. What a movie! *Wuthering Heights* was the movie. A terrible print, a fuzzy soundtrack, a screenplay that probably had Emily Brontë turning in her grave. The backyards of Burbank masquerading as the Yorkshire heath. Corny, hokey, over the top and overblown, it didn't matter. I'll never forget that first shot of him leaning against the fireplace. He made that movie. He changed what I thought acting was all about, and from then on I decided I would be a real actress. No more of this commercial nonsense. Oh, I'd still do it to make money until I got my big break, but I would be a stage actress, a Broadway actress. There was only one problem—I didn't have the slightest idea of how to act on a stage. I'd have to study. . . . I sighed. I hadn't let myself see *Wuthering Heights* since last year. It was too painful.

I tried to communicate all this to Dr. Steinhart. Can anyone ever tell anybody anything and have them understand?

"Who was he?"

I looked at him.

"Laurence Olivier," I said. "That's when I started studying acting . . . after I saw *Wuthering Heights*."

"You hadn't studied before?"

"No. My parents got me started in commercials. My father works in advertising. When I was about five he was working on a commercial for some kind of cereal, I don't even remember what it was. Anyway, my mom and I were supposed to have lunch with him, and we went to pick him up at the set. The director of the commercial saw me and decided to use me in the next one he did. But I never wanted to do them. Well, I guess I thought they were neat when I was little, but it wasn't as if I asked to do them, it just kind of hap-pened. And anyway, I got sick of them pretty soon.

But studying acting, that was something I really wanted to do."

Studying acting. That wasn't something I let myself think about too often anymore. It was way too painful. I didn't know if I missed it or not. Well, actually, I know I didn't miss it, but I still wanted to be on the stage. Maybe what I really missed was having an ambition. I missed the time when I cared about something. Now I felt as if nothing mattered, or ever would again.

"Are you still taking acting classes?"

"Are you crazy? I mean, they're practically the whole reason I'm here!" I trailed off. I didn't want this guy knowing too much. This was the third time that he'd started getting too close, and I didn't want it to be a case of third time lucky. It might have made more sense to just come right out with it and tell him everything. But I couldn't do that. For one thing, I didn't feel like anything would help me, and for another, I guess I felt too guilty. It was my fault that I had ended up like this, and that wasn't something I liked to think about too much. It was easier to stick to the "facts," as he called them. But for the first time in months, I couldn't stop thinking about acting class. Maybe it was for the best that I wasn't taking classes anymore, I mean besides what happened. I know now that my idol

Olivier didn't even approve of the kind of acting I'd been studying.

"You know, it's funny. I went through all this trouble to be able to take acting classes, and then I found out that Olivier really hated the technique I was studying."

"Stephanie, it's time."

It was always time with these bastards. I got up and started struggling with my stuff.

"Stephanie?"

"Hmm?"

"What did you say the kind of acting you were studying was?"

"The method," I said without even thinking. "The sense memory method."

CHAPTER THREE

"Why do you think it's significant that the name of the narrator is never mentioned, yet Rebecca, the dead wife's name, is always coming up, and is even the name of the book?"

Mr. Friedman paused and waited for an answer. I didn't pay any attention. I continued floating in and out of classes, doing what was required of me, or at least what wouldn't raise my parents' suspicions. I couldn't take my mother looking at me with her worried frown anymore, or my father's way of acting bluff and hearty like there wasn't anything wrong. As for my sessions with Dr. Steinhart, they were okay, a place to let off steam, nothing deeper than that.

Mr. Friedman kept talking. Someone asked a question. I didn't bother to listen to the answer. I wasn't worried about doing okay on the quiz, even though I hadn't read the book. Olivier had starred in the movie and it was playing uptown today, so naturally I was planning to go. I looked over at Dahlia; she didn't seem to be listening either. She was the only person I had talked to around school, and that hadn't exactly gone too far.

The bell rang. Everyone grabbed their books and ran out. I always lagged behind, and I was surprised that this time Dahlia did too. She was usually the first out the door.

"Hey, are you going to study hall, or what?" she asked me.

"I guess so, why?"

"Feel like cutting?"

"I don't feel like getting caught."

"You're a good kid, you know that?"

"I'm glad you think so."

"Are you going to get all snotty with me, or what? I'm asking you to cut because I feel like hanging out with you, okay?"

"Okay." Sure. I was flattered, in fact. I didn't know if I'd have anything to say to her after about five minutes, but it was nice to be asked. As for skipping study hall, well, it wasn't the best thing to do, but the chances of getting caught were pretty slim. Besides, wasn't this the kind of thing normal kids did? It sounded so innocent compared to what I'd been through. I knew that even if I were caught I wouldn't get in trouble with my parents. They'd probably be thrilled that I was up to stupid teenage pranks. I could just imagine the conversation.

MY FATHER: Honey, Steph's school just called.

MY MOTHER (face crumpling): Oh no, what now?

MY FATHER: She cut her study hall with some other girl.

MY MOTHER (face wreathed in smiles): She cut a class? With a *friend*? Oh, honey! I'm so happy!

Before I could answer Dahlia, she grabbed my arm and pushed me out the front door.

"Shit," she said under her breath. "Don't look now."

"Huh?"

"You're real swift, you know that? Don't look now, okay?"

"Yeah, sure." There wasn't much to look at anyway. There was an older guy wearing khakis standing across the street, but that was about it.

"You got any money?"

"Some."

"Like how much?"

"About fifty dollars."

"You're kidding! Where'd you get that, you got some rich WASP parents? Huh? Did they just give you your allowance?"

"No," I said coldly. "As a matter of fact, I earned it."

"You're too touchy for your own good, you know that? Ya gotta loosen up."

"How come you wanted to know how much money I have?"

"Look, sweetheart, can you grab a cab before that idiot comes over and starts talking to us?"

"Why should he want to come over here?"

"Because he's my boyfriend."

"Your boyfriend!"

"Hey!" She ignored me and waved her arms at a taxi. "C'mon, get in."

"Where are we going?"

"Did you see the look on his face? Hey, driver, One Hundred and Tenth Street and Amsterdam."

"What's there?"

"A coffee shop."

"All the way uptown? Isn't there one around here?"

"Yeah, but I live up there, and I feel like heading home."

"Okay. I was going uptown anyway. How come you don't go to a school in your neighborhood?" Maybe Dahlia and I had more in common than I thought.

"I used to, but it was really violent. There were a lot of knife fights in the halls, and even the teachers were into drugs. I'm an only kid, and my mom's kind of overprotective. She couldn't afford private school or anything, but she wanted me out of the neighborhood."

That was interesting. None of the girls I used to hang around with before had been onlies. I'd always been a little bit jealous of them. I wondered if Dahlia felt the same way. I don't know why I was starting to think being only children gave us some bond or something. After all, she had a *boyfriend*. As far as I was concerned, boys were totally off-limits—maybe one day when I got my head screwed on straight, if I didn't feel so filthy inside. . . . "Hey, if he's your boyfriend, how come you didn't want to talk to him?"

"Because we had an argument, that's why. I knew he'd try and catch me after school. That's why I wanted to cut. I didn't think he'd figure I'd do that and come early though. I'm glad you were there. I'm not gonna talk to him." She squeezed my arm. "It was great the way we took off, huh? In a cab. Whoo, class, sweetheart!"

"Dahlia?"

"Yeah, what now?"

"Your boyfriend . . . he's, umm, black?" I had been surprised when I saw him, not that I really think anything about that kind of stuff one way or another. But

I never knew anyone in an interracial relationship before. Well, okay, I never really knew anyone in any kind of relationship before. Laurie had dated, I guess, but I never met any of the guys she went out with. And Amy wasn't any readier to be involved with guys than I was. I certainly never knew anyone who was dating someone ten years older. I wondered what Dahlia saw in him. I didn't think he was good-looking at all, whereas she was pretty. When you've been in TV for a while you automatically judge people's looks; it's not the best thing, but I can't help it.

"What are you, a racist or something?" Dahlia snapped. "Listen, little WASP girl, he's not black and neither am I. We're both Puerto Rican, only I'm light-skinned, and he's dark. And so what if he was black, anyway?"

"So nothing. I was just wondering, and I'm not a racist."

"You're some rich snob, right?"

"Will you stop it! You're being just as racist as you think I am. What makes you think I'm rich?"

"Well, you live on the Upper East Side, don't you?"

"How'd you know?"

"I saw it on the cover of your notebook."

"So?"

"Sorry, I just figured you're richer than me."

"What's your boyfriend's name?"

"Daryll."

"I should have figured."

She gave me a look. "Say what?"

"I'm not the only one who writes on notebook covers."

"Oh!" She smiled. "You're okay, you know that?"

"Gee, thanks," I said wryly, but I was pleased. I was also surprised at how easy it was to talk to her.

"Hey," I said, remembering. "He's in the Marines, right?"

"Yup. That's why he was wearing his khakis."

"Does he go away a lot?"

"Well, he's stationed in Brooklyn, but yeah, he goes away a lot, especially to South Carolina. There's a big Marine base down there. Daryll's a private first class—that's better than just being a private," she said proudly.

The taxi stopped and I paid the driver.

"Thanks. I'll pay for the coffee, okay?"

"Sure." The taxi had cost eight dollars.

We went into the coffee shop and sat down.

"What do you want?"

"Just coffee."

"Nothing else?"

"I'm on a diet."

"Why? You don't need to be."

I looked at her. Was she kidding? But she didn't seem like she was laughing at me or anything. I keep forgetting that I'm not a blimp. I'm just somebody who's too heavy to be in commercials anymore, especially with the way the camera adds weight. I suppose I don't really have to lose weight. I noticed Dahlia was waiting for an answer. "Look at my thighs." I figured that any girl no matter how skinny would understand that one, but I was wrong. Dahlia just shook her head.

"You need a Puerto Rican boyfriend. They love big legs."

"What was your argument about?" I didn't want to talk about what kind of boyfriend I needed.

Just then the waitress came, so Dahlia gave our order instead of answering. I waited until the waitress had come back with my coffee and two donuts for Dahlia and asked her again. She licked some powdered sugar from her fingers.

"Let's just say you'll know when I know you better. Hey, you tell me something."

"What?"

"You said you earned your money. Whaddya got, some after-school job or something?"

Should I tell her that I used to do TV commercials?

It might even impress her. But would she even believe me? I kept waiting for someone at school to recognize me. Pathetic but true. I guess I was sort of playing the Gloria Swanson/Bette Davis part. Fading has-been clings to lost aura of stardom, becomes a recluse while at the same time is desperate for people to ask for her autograph. But this time the casting director had really made a mistake. For one thing, I was about fifty years too young for the part, and for another, I was never big enough to make it even to has-been. I decided that even though I was getting along with Dahlia better than I had with anyone else lately, I wasn't going to tell her.

"Let's just say you'll know when I know you better."

She grinned. "You know, I'm getting to like you better all the time. Okay, answer me this one. You said you had to be uptown anyway. What would a kid like you be doing up here?"

"I was planning to see a movie around here."

"Yeah? What movies they got around here that they don't have anywhere else?"

"Well, it's an old movie. There's a theater near here that shows a lot of them."

"An old movie? Like *Raiders of the Lost Ark*? I might come with you."

"*Raiders of the Lost Ark*? I said old!"

"Yeah, so? That's old, right?"

"I mean like fifty or sixty years. At least I think *Rebecca*'s that old."

"*Rebecca*? Does that have anything to do with that book we're reading in English?"

"Uh-huh. It's the same one, all right. That's why I haven't bothered to read the book."

"You're not the only one who hasn't read it. I'm coming with you."

"You might not like it, you know. Besides, I thought you said that you felt like heading home." I was surprised that she wanted to go with me. I mean, cutting was one thing, but going to a movie together? That was something girlfriends did. I was also a little, well, not nervous exactly, but uncomfortable about seeing an Olivier movie with her. For one thing, it's a very personal thing for me to see a movie with him in it. He practically changed my whole life. For another thing, a lot of kids today don't like him, and that makes me really furious. In acting school a lot of the more pretentious students used to carry on about Lord Larry, and say that he was too much of a ham actor. Sure. I bet they would have given their right arm to have been the kind of "ham" actor that he was. In any case, I didn't want to ruin the afternoon by arguing about Olivier with Dahlia.

"I don't care. I have a ton of homework tonight. It'll be great to get *Rebecca* out of the way."

"We better hurry. It's on Ninety-fourth and it starts in half an hour."

"So let's junk this joint. C'mon."

She stood up and I followed her, smiling. The way she talked was different from anyone I'd known before.

I kind of wished I had told her I'd done TV commercials, but then again that might have led to all kinds of questions, like why wasn't I doing them any longer? With someone else I might have made up some excuse, said I got bored or something. But I didn't feel like lying to Dahlia, and I certainly wasn't going to tell the truth. It was weird, because with anyone else I wouldn't have thought twice about making up something. There was something about Dahlia that stopped me, though. I don't know what it was. On the surface she seemed totally confidant, but in some ways she seemed as vulnerable as I was. Maybe I only felt that way because she seemed lonely and wanted my company.

On the way down to Ninety-fourth Street a lot of guys yelled comments at us. I hate that kind of thing, but Dahlia didn't get at all flustered.

"Yo, lady, you got some pretty lips, you know that?"

"I know it and so does my boyfriend!" Dahlia answered.

"You want to see what I got?" some creep yelled, grabbing his crotch.

"Sorry. My mom told me not to play with matches." I giggled self-consciously.

"Hey, lady, you got some good hips. . . ."

"Not you!" he shouted as Dahlia started to answer. "Your friend!"

"See, I told you there were guys who liked real curves." She smiled at me.

"Well, I kind of wish different guys liked them."

"Don't worry, they will."

It was surprising the way she switched from acting really cool to being warm and reassuring. Her vulnerability made her nonthreatening, but it was her reassuring quality that first made me start really liking her.

"This is it, right?"

"Uh, yeah." I dug in my pocket.

"Don't worry, I can pay for myself." She looked around with interest at the faded red velvet curtains and brocade seats. "Boy, this place is something, you know?"

"I know, that's why I love it. There's never anybody here." There were about ten people in the theater as we went in and picked our seats.

"Do you come here a lot?"

"Yup. It depends on what movie they're playing. But I like old movies better than the ones around now."

"Stephanie, hey, Stephanie! Is that you?"

Christ. The last thing I needed. Whoever it was, it was someone I didn't want to see. I thought about not turning around. After all, they could only see the back of my head, maybe they'd think they had the wrong person, but Dahlia would think I was crazy. She was already elbowing me in the ribs.

"What's with you? Someone's calling your name."

I took a deep breath and turned around.

"Stephanie! I can't believe it's you, how are you?"

It couldn't have been worse. A girl from my acting class. Claudia. At least if it had been someone from my old school they might not know the reason why I left. Why couldn't it have been Laurie? I could have complimented her on her lipstick, and gotten out of there, maybe. Or even Amy? Okay, so she was certifiable, but at least she was well meaning, and she was too screwy to say anything that would make much sense. But Claudia? She had been there when things had really fallen apart. She knew about as much of it as anyone did. And she didn't like me either.

"Fine, Claudia," I said shortly. I didn't want to ask

her how she was, what was going on with her, be-cause I didn't want Dahlia to hear her start spouting stuff about acting. I was kind of tongue-tied, but that didn't deter her.

"So how are you really, Stephanie? You look like you've gained weight." She faked an expression of concern. A lot of people have looked at me that way over the past year, and I've gotten really sick of it.

"I told you, great, Claudia." I wished the movie would start. There didn't seem to be any way of get-ting rid of her, in fact, she moved even closer.

She placed her hand on my arm. God, I couldn't believe it. "Really, Steph, the last time I saw you was in class and, well, I always wondered what happened afterward, someone said you'd actually been put in an institution, but I didn't believe that. Still, though, you did seem . . ."

I had to stop her. I would die if she said any more. I don't mean that as a figure of speech, I mean that lit-erally, I would shrivel up and die. Wasn't I ever going to be over it? Today was the first time I had talked to someone for more than five minutes who wasn't a shrink, it was the first time I'd gone to the movies with someone in more than a year, and this had to happen. I had to stop her from saying any more, though she'd already done enough damage. Dahlia would think I was a freak. I wanted the floor to swallow me up. I couldn't think of anything to say.

"I, well, look . . ." I was stumbling over my own words, trying to say something, anything that would get rid of her. It was obvious I was having a hard time, and to anyone but Claudia, it would have been obvious that I didn't want to talk to her.

"Wow, you really do seem pretty shaken up, Stephanie." Claudia used my discomfiture as evidence that I was still one step away from the loony bin.

"I think Stephanie's not that interested in talking to you, or can't you figure that out for yourself?" I was shocked to hear Dahlia come to my rescue.

"Excuse me?" Apparently Claudia was pretty surprised too.

"I said, I don't think she wants to talk to you, and I certainly don't. Shoo, girl, anyone ever tell you you wear way too much perfume? By the way, anybody who looks like you do in those pants shouldn't be telling someone else they've gained weight." Dahlia reached out and grabbed the label on the back of Claudia's jeans. "Size eight? That's pretty impressive, girl! I mean, it's pretty hard for a size twelve to stuff herself into a size eight! How'd you do it?"

That did it. Claudia flounced off. Dahlia plonked down in her seat with a satisfied smile on her face. I kept standing. I was so shocked. No one had ever stood up for me like that before. Dahlia didn't even know me that well, but she was willing to do that for me. It was almost like she was aligning herself with me. Us against them, whoever "them" might be. Impatiently, Dahlia grabbed my sleeve and pulled me down into the seat next to her.

"What's with you? Don't you want to see the movie?"

Now that I had had a moment to digest what Dahlia had done, I was starting to feel frightened. What must she think about what Claudia had said?

"Umm, Dahlia, listen, I used to know that girl and she, well, she . . ." What could I say? That Claudia had made the whole thing up?

"Forget it, man, anyone could see that chick had it in for you. What was that jazz she was going on about, anyway? You should have told her where to stick it."

I couldn't believe it. Dahlia didn't really get what Claudia had been saying. I was so relieved, I figured I probably shouldn't say anything else about it, except . . . "Dahlia?"

"Yeah?"

"Thanks for getting rid of her."

Dahlia grinned at me. "Hey, you helped me get

away from Daryll this afternoon, I figured I owed you."

The lights went down and I sat back in my seat. I was thinking about what had just happened more than I was watching the movie, but after about ten minutes Dahlia nudged my elbow.

"Psst."

"What?"

"Who's that?"

"Who?"

"Him." She pointed at the screen.

"That's just a waiter."

"No! Him—the guy sitting down."

"That's Max De Winter. Haven't you even opened the book?"

"No, I mean who is he?"

The few people in the theater started making shushing noises. I was betting Claudia would call the manager if we didn't stop.

"Well?"

"Shhh! I told you, Max De Winter."

"I MEAN WHAT ACTOR, DUMMY!"

"BE QUIET!" someone yelled. I shrank down in my seat.

"Are you going to answer?" Dahlia whispered.

"That's Laurence Olivier."

"Oh."

I started watching the movie again, but after about ten minutes Dahlia nudged me again.

"What now?"

"Sweetheart, that man is drop-dead gorgeous."

I looked at her. She was staring straight ahead and practically drooling, and I realized that I had found a friend.

CHAPTER FOUR

I'd been seeing Dr. Steinhart for about three weeks, and so far my sessions hadn't gotten into anything really heavy-duty. That was fine with me, but psychs aren't happy unless they get you to "open up." Actually, that's only if they care enough to bother. They sure didn't at Pleasantville. The social worker assigned to me there couldn't have cared less if I didn't say a word the whole session. Dr. Stevenson hadn't cared that much toward the end either. So far Rob had been pretty good, though. I hadn't even seen expression number twelve yet, and I was pushing it, too. I hardly ever said anything unless he asked me a direct question. I knew from experience that shrinks hated that; they wanted you to do all the talking so that they could sit back and relax. Usually when I showed up at Dr. Steinhart's, I just sat and stared at him until he got bored of looking at me, and started talking. There was only one problem with this method, though— he tended to ask more serious stuff than I wanted to answer. Like today, after our staring contest was over, he went right for the jugular.

"So much has changed for you this year," he said, "and it would be very natural if you missed your old routine—acting, for instance." He paused and waited for an answer. He could wait forever before I answered that one. Even though I liked Dr. Steinhart better than any of the other psychs I'd been to, the whole bunch of them made me sick sometimes. Even if I did "open up," as soon as I spilled my guts Rob would tell me that our session was over. I can't keep my emotions on a time clock like that. It's easier not to open up at all. Besides, I've never talked about it with anyone. My parents knew what had happened, at least in a roundabout way. How could they not? When my acting teacher had brought me home after my "episode" they'd grilled him pretty hard. Still, except for a few tentative forays at Pleasantville on visiting day, we'd never cleared the air about it. I knew they were dying to ask me what Rob said about the whole thing. I'm sure that it never occurred to them that I was avoiding the issue with my therapist. Of course they would think that I'd be anxious to talk about it, to "come clean," so to speak. Only with this there was no coming clean.

"I'm sorry if this seems painful, Stephanie," Dr.

Steinhart continued, interrupting my thoughts. "But I'm just fishing, trying to hit anything that will help you get started. We've barely gone into the events of last year, and that's important stuff. If it seems like I'm pushing you, it's only to help you get going."

I didn't say anything. For one thing, I didn't have anything to say, and for another, I felt bad—I mean, he was really trying to get through to me. Part of me wanted to help him out a little, but the rest of me just couldn't.

"Let's start with something fairly straightforward, okay?" He leaned forward, resting his elbows on his knees. Boy, he even had the right gestures; this was a perfect pose to complement the number five look. "Why did your parents want you to stop studying acting? After all, as you said, they originally pushed you into acting, didn't they?"

If he thought the answer to that one was straightforward, he had another thing coming.

"'Fairly straightforward,' huh? You're really swift, you know that? I mean, the reason my parents made me stop is practically the whole reason I'm here, isn't it?" I couldn't stop myself from being sarcastic. The guy should have figured out some things about my situation.

"Stephanie, I can't know these things unless you

tell me. I wonder if you realize just how recalcitrant you are. I've rarely worked with someone less forthcoming than you. You understand, of course, that even though your parents arranged our sessions, we didn't discuss you apart from the most cursory medical history. So if you don't talk to me about what's going on with you, I can't know. After all, I'm not a mind reader."

His delivery was perfect. I doubt Olivier could have done it better. I figured that he had a point, and I decided to try and be a little more cooperative. I thought about the fact that my parents had made me stop studying acting. Of course, I couldn't have continued anyway, especially not at the same school, not after what had happened, but I do wish it had been my decision, instead of by default. All of a sudden I felt angry. I realized I never had any say in anything. That's probably why I never said anything in these stupid sessions, just so I could have some control somewhere. It occurred to me that every time I stared Rob down it was my way of jerking him like a puppet on a string. But so what? The more I thought about it, the more it seemed futile to even try and talk about things with him.

"What does it matter whether I tell you anything or not?" I muttered angrily. "What I say doesn't matter."

"I don't understand what makes you say that. I'm interested in anything you have to say."

"Well, you're the only one, then." I was angry now. Maybe Rob listened to me, but that was only because he was paid to. "It doesn't matter whether I tell you anything, because things aren't up to me, are they? My parents decided I should stop acting, they decided I should go to a new school, too; they even found you. Well, you know what really makes me mad? All this time my parents are running around trying to fix things, they're ignoring the real issue. They don't even think about their part in this. And you know what's even worse?" I paused to take a breath. Poor Rob looked pretty surprised at how loudly I was shouting. "The worst part is that they think I'm the one to blame, they think everything's my fault. They think that none of this stuff would have happened if I hadn't decided to be a real actress." I stopped, surprised that I had said so much to him. I was surprised by what I had said, too. Didn't I agree with my parents? Wasn't that at least part of the problem, that I thought I was the one to blame too? Of course, I thought it was my fault for other reasons than my parents had. But maybe I wasn't the only bad guy.

"Stephanie, it's hard for me to know what to say; I don't know much about your reasons for being in therapy. You've been very closed-mouthed until now, and even though you just revealed some feelings, I'm largely left in the dark about certain issues. What do you mean your parents have a part in this? What's 'this'? I'm also confused about the connection that you make between being a 'real' actress and your emotional problems. You need to clarify these things, not just for me, but in your own mind too. I'm very curious about what's going on with you. Clearly you're here for a host of reasons, but it's just as clear that there's one overriding issue. Do you think you can use that as your starting-off point? Are you willing to talk about that?" He paused for a second, but when I didn't say anything, he continued. "About your feeling that your parents are to blame, let me just say that in twenty-five years of therapy I've yet to see that assigning blame has ever helped anyone. Clearly you have a lot of anger toward your parents, and we need to work through that, as well as why you have that anger to begin with. At the same time, though, I think you need to address this issue of deciding whose fault your problems are. It's certainly possible that other people can sometimes do things that have profound effects on us, but while those acts can be hard to forgive, it's necessary for your own survival to take responsibility for your life."

Great. Now he sounded just like Dr. Stevenson. Would he finally give me a number twelve? We were both quiet for a while, then:

"Stephanie?"

"Yeah, I know, it's time."

"That's true," Dr. Steinhart said, "but I was going to say that I'm glad you said what you did, there's a lot of things we have to explore, but I feel like you've started the ball rolling."

"See you next week," I said as he closed the door behind me.

I decided to walk across the park on my way home from Dr. Steinhart's. My parents hated it when I did that. They thought it was dangerous. For the first time it occurred to me that when I did things they didn't like, I was trying to punish them.

I thought about what I'd told, or rather hadn't told, Dr. Steinhart in my session. I'd been pretty clear about how angry I was about my parents, but not much else. I'd never told him why I "fell apart," so to speak. Maybe because I was a little confused about all the details myself. There were the obvious things like the pressure of trying to be a "real" actress. And of course all the other students in acting school really disliked me. I mean, who was I to have made all this money from commercials when they had all this talent and had to wait tables to pay the rent—most of the other acting students were in their twenties, and really struggling financially. But even though things like that can be wearing, I'm not the kind of person to fall apart because I'm not winning any popularity contests. So what really did it? To tell the truth, I knew what it was. It was the sense memory.

Sense memory. Just saying the words was enough to bring it all back. That's part of why I'd never told Dr. Steinhart about it—I never wanted to experience anything that awful again. Another reason was that it was just too bizarre. I'm not sure he'd even believe me.

I don't know what I was expecting when I first started studying acting. I guess I just thought I'd learn monologues. Shakespeare, Ibsen, stuff like that. Well, I was wrong.

"All right, everybody, sit in your chairs and relax," my teacher Jim said. These chairs were pretty special too, not exactly the kind you'd choose to relax in. "Create your circle of attention. It should be a circle of light. Once you've created it, it's impenetrable, and you'll banish all thoughts from your mind."

Okay. Not too hard to understand—it just sounds a little metaphysical, that's all. Obviously, I'm just supposed to concentrate on relaxing. As for this circle of light, I guess he just means a barrier.

"We'll start relaxing from the feet up. When you feel tension, send a message from the brain to the area, telling it to relax."

The power of positive thinking, huh? I'm a little skeptical, but what the hell.

"Tension is the actor's worst enemy," he went on. "It impedes the flow of creativity; your body is your instrument and you must learn to control it. When we are completely relaxed, we will begin the sensory work."

I opened my eyes.

"What's your name?" Jim asked.

"Stephanie."

"Well, Stephanie, you have no concentration. Zero, zilch, nada, understand? I broke your circle just like that." He snapped his fingers.

"I'm sorry, but what's sensory work? I don't know how to do it yet. Did you explain it before?"

"Close your eyes and re-create your circle. You'll understand the sensory work when it's time for you to. All right, everybody, you're relaxed, you're concentrated, and now you're ready to start the work. I want you all to create a coffee cup. How does the cup feel? Is it hot? How much does it weigh? How does your coffee smell? You must re-create the coffee sensorily—in other words, through the sense of smell, touch, taste, et cetera."

Well, that didn't sound too hard. I guess I was supposed to mime it, that's all. I didn't quite understand the way he phrased it, all this re-creating of senses and stuff.

So I started to imagine a coffee cup. In a way I was aggravated. I knew nothing about mime and was having a hard time doing it. All of a sudden I felt a hand on my arm.

"That's enough for today, you can quit now," Jim said.

I watched the other people who were still up there. It was more than a little weird, everybody looked as if they were in a trance, holding imaginary coffee cups.

One by one Jim made everyone stop, and then we sat around in a circle while he talked.

"You're probably all a little freaked out by this, I can tell. Good. That's the way we like you to feel. That's one of the reasons why we don't explain the sense memory at first, just kind of throw you in. Okay. So you're wondering, what is this sense memory bullshit? If I tell you it's also called memory of emotion, will that help clear it up?" He looked around, nobody said anything. "Well, I'm glad that helped," he joked.

"The sense memory is the tool that will help you release your talent. It is the key to your inner emotions. First, it helps you develop your imagination. Can you really create an object without it being there? Can you re-create the smell of coffee through your senses? The object of these exercises is not to mime," he said, looking at me, "but to be able to expand your imagination to create a reality that is nonexistent. When you're in a play in which the scene requires that you've just come in from the cold, but it's ninety-two degrees outside and the only place you're coming from is dusty old backstage, how do you get the feeling of the cold? By the sense memory, that's how," he said, answering his own question.

"So you mean this stuff is going to help me be a better Ophelia, for instance?" I piped up.

Jim gave me a look. "Why are you worried?"

Huh? What's with this guy? "I'm not worried."

"Yes, you are. You're worried about the result. Will this really work? Will this help you get a job? You can't worry about those things now. You're not ready to be Ophelia yet."

"I wasn't worried about getting a job," I said, embarrassed.

"You're worried about the result, though, about whether you can really do this. Don't worry, you're not the only one," he said, relenting when he saw how embarrassed I was.

"Honestly, I wasn't. I just don't understand how this works, that's all."

"You'll understand more when you're ready. Right now you've got to build up your concentration and create the coffee, not worry about how, what, or why."

Well, okay, none of this sounds that earthshaking. I mean really, falling apart trying to imagine a coffee cup? But there's more to the sense memory than that, and as I began to "be ready," as Jim put it, I learned.

The way you "expand your imagination" is fairly straightforward. After all, if you can really taste your morning coffee or be able to put sunshine all over your body when it's raining outside (another sense memory), I'd say your imagination is getting pretty good. The other part of the sense memory is a little insidious, though. Stanislavsky, the creator of the sense memory method, was friends with Pavlov. I'd read about Pavlov freshman year. He was a scientist. The one who every time he fed his dogs would ring a little bell. The dogs knew they were going to get this nice red juicy meat, so of course they'd start to drool. But after a while Pavlov would just ring the bell, and they'd drool anyway because they'd associate the bell ringing with the meat, whether they got it or not.

Well, when you do the sense memory, all these feelings start to come up. For instance, the sunshine made me feel really shy. I don't know why it did—as Jim said, it doesn't matter why. The first time I did the sunshine it took forty-five minutes to really feel it, the next time it took about half an hour, by the fifth time I could get the sunshine and the shyness that went with it in five minutes.

Well, here's where Pavlov comes in for the actor: eventually you get to the point where you say *sunshine* to yourself and the sunshine comes up in a second. Pretty neat if you're in a play and you have to feel shy all of a sudden.

Still doesn't seem like the type of thing to drive somebody over the edge? Maybe not, but I know one thing. It's not just stuff like shyness that comes up. All the feelings you've suppressed all your life start to erupt, things you'd rather not have come up, like every bad memory you've ever had and every nightmare rolled into one. I know another thing too. They really teach you how to turn this stuff on in acting school. There's just one problem: they don't tell you how to turn it off.

CHAPTER FIVE

"Say, girl, where you been? You got some secret or something?"

It was Tuesday, and Dahlia had cornered me after English class. We had become buddies since that day at the movies. It was all kind of new for me to have someone to pal around with, but ever since she stood up for me against Claudia, Dahlia seemed to take it for granted that we would stick together. If it had been up to me I wouldn't have known how to continue things, but as it was, it had been pretty natural the way we'd started hanging out with each other. We'd taken to talking on the phone every night. The first time she'd called I thought my mother would faint.

"There's someone on the phone for you," my mother said in the kind of voice she might use to announce that I'd won the lottery.

"C'mon, Mom, I'm not a leper. It's not that rare for someone to call me." But it was, and we both knew it.

My mother hovered around nervously while I talked to Dahlia.

"How'd you get my number?"

"You ever hear of the phone book?"

"Did you want the homework for English?" I couldn't figure out why'd she'd call otherwise.

"What are you, crazy? Listen, I wanted to ask you, did you catch that outfit that Delmore was wearing today? I thought the guys were going to go crazy. I mean, I know she's young, but hey, she is a teacher. She shouldn't be wearing stuff like that."

Dahlia continued about the propriety of Ms. Delmore's wardrobe. I just propped my chin in my hand and listened. This was what normal kids did, I guessed. Well, it sure was better than someone calling to tell me that they had gotten the commercial that I had been called back for five times. And it definitely beat the hell out of Amy showing me the slash marks on her wrist. The only friend I'd ever had before who came close to being like Dahlia was Laurie. And even though I used to have fun with her, there was always an undercurrent of tension between us. After all, even though we were different types, we did sometimes go up for the same commercials. But things were different with Dahlia. More relaxed. Sometimes I felt uncomfortable with her—I was always on my guard against saying something that I shouldn't, but for the most part it was pretty easy. Take this phone call for instance, it was soothing to listen to Dahlia talk, it took my mind off my own problems. I purposely avoided my mother's eyes after we hung up. I knew she was burning with curiosity. Well, let her wonder, I wasn't about to tell her anything.

"I feel like I haven't seen you in days," Dahlia said to me now as we stood in the hall. I'd gone over to her house last Friday after my session with Rob. That had been a first for me too. I couldn't ever remember going over to a girlfriend's house in the past, unless you counted the times that Laurie and I used to get ready for auditions together. Dahlia and I had just hung out together channel surfing. I'd been kind of nervous. What if an old commercial with me on it came up? But Dahlia had only half an eye on the TV anyway. She'd been more interested in talking about Daryll.

"I don't understand what you're talking about. We saw each other three days ago." I felt like an idiot when I said that. It sounded really cold. After the past year of doing nothing but thinking about myself, I wasn't always as sensitive as I could be. But Dahlia took it in stride.

"Oooh, so formal." She rolled her eyes at me. "Listen, who are you trying to kid here? Half the time you're never in study hall, and I know you're not cool enough to be cutting without me. You got some mystery lover?"

"I wish." I'd wondered when she'd call me on the fact that I missed a lot of study halls. I guess I should be grateful that it hadn't come up before now, at least we'd had some time to get to know each other before she found out about the real me and got scared off.

"So what's the deal? You got too many secrets, you know that?"

"What secrets do I have?" I asked innocently, but I was playing for time.

"Well, you won't tell me where you go instead of study hall. I mean, like last Friday, why couldn't you have come straight home with me from school? Why were you so hush-hush about why you couldn't get together until after five? And how come you're always loaded? You don't have an after-school job, and you say your parents don't give you any money. C'mon, tell the truth, you doing a little hooking on the side?"

"Dahlia!" I couldn't help laughing. "You're crazy!"

"Tell me something I don't know. Look, are you going to let me in on this, or what?"

I'd been asking myself the same question for a few days now. I knew that sooner or later Dahlia was going to start putting two and two together and coming up with five. There was no way I was going to tell her what I hadn't told Dr. Steinhart. But I didn't want to just shrug her questions off, either. It had been pretty hard for me at school since I'd been back. I don't mean academically or anything like that. I just felt dirty somehow, like people could look right through me and see all the scars that were inside. I wanted to know what would happen if somebody really saw the scars. Would they still talk to me? Would they think I was some kind of freak or something? But I needed to confide in someone, just a little. I wanted to let down my guard. I wanted to let Dahlia know just a little bit of the real me. Maybe I couldn't tell her all about the me that was so screwed up, but I could tell her something about the me that used to be. I took a deep breath.

"Well, okay. It's pretty tame, actually." Well, the part of the story that I was going to tell her was, and even if she knew the whole thing, I still think it didn't compare to hooking.

"Listen, if I'm going to be hearing true confessions I don't want to be hanging around the hall. Let's go sit in the park."

"I thought a lot of drug dealers hang around there." Dahlia was definitely a "just say no" kind of girl. I thought my parents were overprotective, but they were like Hell's Angels compared to Dahlia's mom. I'd stayed for dinner on Friday and gotten pretty seriously grilled about everything, from where I lived to how my parents had voted in the last election. On the way home I wondered how Dahlia handled having a mom that strict. Then I realized that going out with someone like Daryll was probably her way of dealing with it.

"Drug dealers are the safest people to be around. Didn't you know that? They're too interested in making money to try anything with you. Besides, there's always a lot of cops around trying to buy some good pot or something."

"Did anyone ever tell you that you're pretty cynical?" I teased her, but the truth was, I loved her sarcastic sense of humor.

"Do me a favor, okay? Don't pull any attitude on me."

We walked outside into the park. It was a pretty place if you ignored all the scummy people hanging around. We sat under a tree. It was October and the leaves were falling all around us. Dahlia closed her eyes and leaned back against a tree.

"Two rules, all right? One, make it juicy. Two, lie if it isn't."

I wasn't going to indulge her with the juicy part. I figured I'd just start with the easy stuff, the "facts," as

Dr. Steinhart liked to call them.

"So come on," Dahlia prodded. "Why aren't you in study hall half the time?"

"Well, the reason that I skip study hall so often is that I go to my psychiatrist on those days. The only time he had available conflicted with study hall, so they let me leave early. That's also why I couldn't come over last Friday right away. My session doesn't end until four forty-five, so I couldn't get to your house until around five-thirty." I wasn't that nervous about telling her this part. After all, a lot of New York kids go to shrinks.

"You go to a head doctor?"

"Yep."

"How come? I mean, you're definitely weird, but you're not in la-la land or anything."

Well, I was glad she didn't think I was. I certainly had my own doubts. Now for the hard part. "Well, my parents think I am." I paused. I could tell that she was going to say that everybody's parents thought they were crazy. And now that I was really telling her about myself, I didn't just want her to brush it all off. That would trivialize it somehow. "To tell you the truth," I plunged on before I could change my mind, "it's not just my parents' bullshit. I really did have some serious problems."

Dahlia opened her eyes at that. "So what's wrong with you?" She said it in the same jaunty way she said most things, but I could tell she was trying to be careful of my feelings.

"It's hard for me to talk about, I don't really know how to put it. I guess the simplest explanation was that I got messed up last year. I had to leave school in January."

"Is that what that creep was going on about?"

"Huh?" I was shocked. Had someone been talking about me?

"You know, that girl who wore too much perfume. She said the last time she had seen you was in class, and that she wondered where you'd gone."

I was white with fear. So Dahlia really had been paying attention to what Claudia had said. "You mean you heard what she was saying?" I trailed off. Had Dahlia been thinking all this time that I had been in an institution or something?

"Oh, no, I didn't want to upset you. Look, of course I heard what she was going on about. I'm not deaf, and I'm not exactly an idiot either. I just figured you'd tell me what she was talking about when you wanted to. I mean, anyone could see that you were pretty uncomfortable back then. I didn't want to push you. I figured you have your feelings, you know?"

Dahlia was blushing. "Anyway, you seemed like you were starting to tell me, so I figured it wouldn't hurt if I mentioned it. So c'mon, what happened?"

In a way the fact that Dahlia had known all along meant more to me than her standing up for me in the first place. It had been a while since we'd seen the movie, and in all that time she'd never pressed me to tell her anything. She hadn't thought I was too weird to hang out with. She'd known my secret—well, at least she'd sort of known—and she'd kept it to herself. More than anything else, that made me feel like I could trust her.

"I guess I sort of had a nervous breakdown." Actually, I didn't have to guess, I knew. And it wasn't "sort of," it was about as full-fledged as they come.

"You're kidding! Erica had one of those on *All My Children!*"

"Yeah, well, mine was a little less glamorous than that."

"And you got to leave school because of that?"

I nodded.

"Was that fun? I mean, did you get to go shopping all the time and stuff?"

I thought about last January. First I'd been at Pleasantville. That had only lasted two weeks, thank God. My parents had removed me when they saw how terrible it was. I mean, it was like some nightmare out of a Charles Dickens novel. They hadn't known quite what to do with me after that. It was clear that I needed help, but they figured a return to my regular routine would probably make things easier. So I'd gone back to school after the Christmas break. I lasted one day. The principal had to get my mother to come and pick me up. After that came the thrilling search for a therapist. With Dr. Marks I'd gone five times a week. The sessions hadn't done a lot for me headwise, but they did break up the monotony of staying in bed all day. Shopping all the time? That didn't quite describe it.

"Well, not exactly. I was pretty much out of it most of the time."

"So what did you do between January and September?"

"That girl we ran into at the movie theater heard right."

"Huh?"

"She said that she'd heard that I was in an institution. She was right." Talk about your melodramatic delivery! Even Joan Crawford had never sounded that pathetic in *What Ever Happened to Baby Jane?* I tried to get the quaver out of my voice, but I couldn't. It was also pretty hard to look at Dahlia.

"Was it awful?" She sounded pretty subdued her-self, but not like she was about to run off or anything.

"It was the worst. I think if I'd had to stay there for any longer than I did, I would've gotten even cra-zier. But I was there only for two weeks."

"Did they, you know, put you in a straitjacket or anything?"

I almost smiled at that one. No, they hadn't put me in a straitjacket or anything. Only people like Joanne Woodward got those in movies like *The Three Faces of Eve*.

"No, it wasn't like that. It was just that nobody cared." It was more than that, really. It was that I was left alone with my own thoughts too much of the time. Two weeks with nothing to do but remember how my whole world had just blown up in my face. I'd get checked out by the resident doc every other day, but that only took about ten minutes. Most of the time I was on my own, when more than ever I needed to be surrounded by other people, to be diverted. I used to do a monologue in acting class about a girl who had nothing to do but "lie awake, and watch her body try to breathe." That's what Pleasantville was like. The only thing I did was lie awake and watch my body try to breathe. That, and think about what had brought me there in the first place. Boy, if I ever get a chance to do that monologue again, I'll nail it.

"But you were only there for two weeks, so what did you do the rest of the time?"

"I saw two shrinks."

"Both at the same time?"

"No." I couldn't help smiling. "I went to this one shrink, Dr. Marks, but it didn't really work out with her, so then I went to another for a while. That wasn't too great either."

"So who are you going to now?"

"Dr. Steinhart. He's pretty okay, I guess." I was surprised I'd said that. I'd never really thought about it before, but it was true. He was definitely better than the others.

"Okay, so now I know why you're never in study hall, but what made you crack up to begin with?"

She was starting to get too close for comfort now. I couldn't let her in on this part. Not yet anyway. She must have seen the look on my face because she changed the subject.

"Hey, I'm sorry if that sounded kind of harsh. Listen, tell me something else I'm dying to know. Where'd you get all your money from?"

I guess Dahlia had heard enough about my shrinks. That was fine with me. I could deal with talking about something else, but could I really tell her how I'd gotten my money? Commercials had always been a barrier between me and other kids before. The kids at my acting school resented me for doing them, and the kids at my regular school, well, let's just say I always stuck out. Like I told Dr. Steinhart, the switch to public school was to give me a shot at being anonymous for a change. Still, Dahlia hadn't been too freaked out by my whole nervous breakdown/shrink experience. Maybe she'd be able to handle this, too. All of a sudden I had an idea. I looked at my watch. My mother had mentioned that she was getting together with friends that afternoon, and I knew she wouldn't be home for another couple hours. As for my father, he'd be at work until at least five-thirty. Perfect. I didn't want to have to deal with them meeting Dahlia.

"C'mon." I stood up, brushing the leaves from my jeans.

"Where are we going?"

"It's a surprise. C'mon."

I hailed a cab at the corner and bundled Dahlia into it. I gave the driver my home address before I had time to change my mind.

"What's going on?" Dahlia asked.

"You'll see." The cab pulled up outside my building.

"Hey, Pete," I said to the doorman. "Is my mother around?"

"No, Stephie, she went out."

Pete always called me Stephie. I didn't mind—he'd known me my whole life. He looked almost as surprised as my parents would have at my having a friend over. Well, why wouldn't he? After all, he'd seen me the day they brought me home from acting class.

"Do you want something to drink?" I asked as I let us into the apartment.

Dahlia shrugged. "I could handle a Coke." She looked around. "This place is huge!"

I nodded. I guess we do have a pretty big apartment, especially compared to Dahlia's. I hoped she wouldn't feel awkward about it or anything. Dahlia's parents weren't divorced, but in her words her father had been a "no-show" since she'd been a kid. I knew her mother worked really hard as a legal secretary, but that didn't spell Park Avenue. I felt guilty that financially I'd always had it easy. Dahlia had to make sacrifices that I would never have even thought of. She couldn't afford a lot of stuff that I would have liked to do together. I wouldn't have minded paying, but it wasn't that easy. Dahlia was proud.

We went into the kitchen and grabbed some sodas. Dahlia stared open-mouthed at everything. "Let's go," I said, pulling her toward my room. Now that I'd made up my mind, I was impatient.

"Are you going to let me in on what's happening, or what?" Dahlia sat down on my bed.

"Just give me one sec," I went into my closet and got down some tapes. What should I put in? I took the one labeled 14–16 and popped it into the VCR. "This is why I'm 'loaded all the time,' as you put it. It's also related to why I'm messed up." That was true. I wouldn't have any money if I'd never done commercials. And if I hadn't done commercials, I would have never studied acting. And if I'd never studied acting . . .

"Hey, girl, where'd you go?" Dahlia snapped her fingers in front of my face.

"Sorry, I was just drifting."

"So you were saying?" Dahlia prompted me.

"The reason I have money is kind of the reason I see a shrink now."

"Hey, I didn't hit on anything with the hooking, did I? Because I was just kidding."

"Dahlia! Will you stop!" I hit the Play button on the remote. I didn't even remember what was on this particular tape. I hadn't watched them in a long time. I leaned back against the pillows, and waited for the first one to run.

"Did you rent some movie with that actor you like?" Dahlia asked.

"Just watch, okay?"

"That's you!" Dahlia shrieked.

"Umm-hmm." Boy, I looked so different then! It wasn't just the weight, or the hair, or any of that stuff. It was that I looked happy. I looked like I was genuinely glad to be eating M&M's. I remembered that commercial: it had taken forever! I think we had to do fifty takes of the opening shot, and every time we did, I had to start with a new package of M&M's. I couldn't audition for anything else for a few weeks, because I'd broken out so much. The screen faded and a spot for Swiss Miss came on. Dahlia looked transfixed.

"You're famous!" she shrieked again.

"Hardly." She seemed really impressed, though. I didn't know what was wrong with me, I should have been happy that Dahlia was reacting the way she was. But all of a sudden things seemed so sad. There I was on the screen about to apply for my first summer job at McDonald's, and here I was in my room, with my life fallen apart around me. I couldn't help it. I started to cry.

"What's wrong with you? What's the problem?" Dahlia looked surprised and confused. I shrugged my shoulders, but I didn't know how to answer her.

"How come you never told me about this stuff before?" Dahlia waved her hand at the TV screen.

"I don't know." I sniffed. "That part of my life is over. You just wanted to know where I got my money from, so I figured I'd show you." Okay, maybe part of me had wanted to impress Dahlia too. Maybe I wanted to show her that I wasn't always a loser.

"You must have made a lot of money doing this, right? How many commercials did you do? How did you get started? Maybe I saw you before and just don't remember!"

"Slow down." I smiled through my tears.

"Well?"

"Okay, I didn't make a fortune or anything. It's not like I can pay for college, but I do have some spending money socked away." I had quite a bit, actually, but I wanted to downplay it for Dahlia's sake.

"Go on, tell me the rest! How many did you do?"

"Umm, let me think for a sec." I didn't want to sound blasé about it, but since I'd been doing them since I was five, it took me a while to sort it all out. "I don't know exactly. My first one was for toothpaste; I got that one by luck. Then I kind of went through a dry spell for a while. I did a whole bunch of cereal commercials. You just saw one of my McDonald's spots. I had a couple of those. My agent used to joke that you weren't really a teenager until you'd done a fast-food commercial. What else? I always wanted to book a shampoo job, but I used to have short hair, and that isn't really the look for that. I don't know, I guess maybe I've done about twelve or fourteen, but remember, that breaks down to about one a year." Dahlia looked thoughtful as she digested all of this.

"Was it fun?"

"Sometimes. There's a lot of competition, and when you do land a spot it can be really boring. There's a joke in TV that acting is just waiting around. I mean, you have to get up at five A.M. to get ready, and then you stand around for hours until they get all the lights right. After that you say 'Nestlé's makes the very best' about four hundred times in a row. But, yeah, it was fun sometimes." At least it had been at one point, when I didn't know enough to want anything else.

"So how did doing commercials mess you up?"

"Well, it wasn't that direct, they were just kind of the first step." Should I tell her what I hadn't told Dr. Steinhart?

"I don't get you! Somebody puts me on TV and pays me for it, I'm going to be happy, not get all screwed up!"

Suddenly I wished I hadn't told her. I guess what I was thinking must have shown on my face, because Dahlia looked sorry.

"Listen, I don't know what I'm talking about. Maybe I'd get messed up too. I mean, I get screwed up just hanging around with Daryll."

"How do you get messed up with Daryll?" I was glad the spotlight was off me for a while.

"Well, my mother likes to give me problems about it. You saw how strict she is. She hates it that he's ten years older than me. She really wishes we'd break up, but she can't do anything about it. I mean, if Daryll was into drugs, that would be it, but he's a Marine, so she knows he's clean. Part of the reason I never, you know, go too far fooling around with Daryll is because I don't want to give my mother grounds for splitting us up. Sometimes I think she's right, though. Maybe he is too old for me, and we don't exactly get to see each other that often, either. What do you think?"

"I'm not the best person to ask about boyfriend stuff," I said slowly. "But did you ever think that maybe your going out with Daryll was just a way of acting out? I mean, your mom does keep you on a pretty tight leash." I sounded a little like Dr. Steinhart, but what the hell.

Dahlia looked thoughtful. "I guess maybe it might have started out that way, but now I really care about him. It's just that sometimes it gets difficult; I feel pulled between him and my mom."

"It sounds like you could use a shrink too. Not that I think you're messed up or anything," I said quickly when I saw the look on her face. "It's just that some' times it's good to talk about this kind of stuff with someone."

Dahlia gave me a strange look. "That's what I have you for. Listen, I got to get going." She stood up and stretched. "I'm really glad you showed me this stuff," she said shyly, waving her hand at the VCR. "I thought maybe you didn't like me that much, you know? You always seemed to have some secret that you wouldn't share."

Well, she still didn't know the half of it, but I was amazed that she thought I didn't like her. I felt closer to her than I did to just about anyone else.

I walked Dahlia to the elevator, and carried our soda glasses into the kitchen. It was dark by now, and my parents still weren't home. I went back to my room and laid down on the bed. I was glad that I'd told Dahlia as much as I had, and I was also glad that she didn't push things too far, asking about how commer' cials had screwed me up. I was drained emotionally from the afternoon, though, and I let myself drift off to sleep instead of thinking too much.

"Stephanie?" My mother poked her head in the

room. I looked at the clock; I'd been out for about an hour. "Dinner's ready, honey."

I followed my mother into the kitchen. She had a purposeful look on her face that I couldn't quite figure out.

"Stephanie," she said in a serious tone, "there were two glasses in the sink."

I looked at her blankly. It wasn't like my mother to get upset over the fact that I hadn't washed a couple of glasses.

"Stephanie, did you drink out of two glasses, or did you have someone over here?"

Oh, so that was it, my mother the detective. She kills me. She probably thought she was being really suave, kind of like Humprey Bogart/Sam Spade, only it wasn't coming off quite that way.

"How's my best girl?" my father said, coming into the room.

I hate it when my father talks that way. He used to call me his best girl when I was five years old. Ever since everything fell apart last year he's started doing it again. What did he think? That if he pretended I was a little kid again he could make what happened go away?

"Stephanie had a friend over," my mother announced to my father.

"This Dr. Steinhart must be doing a good job," my father said.

I can't stand comments like that. What did my father mean? That I was some kind of charity case that no one would like to make friends with, but that Dr. Steinhart had managed to make me acceptable?

"So what friend is this?" my mother asked a little too casually.

"Look, you guys don't have to worry about losing track or anything, it's not like I have a thousand."

"Stephanie," my mother sighed. "I wish you wouldn't be so hostile. We're glad to see you making friends, that's all. Is this the girl that you've been talking with on the phone lately?"

I looked down at the floor. I felt a little ashamed that I'd snapped at my parents. It seemed like that was the only way I could talk to them anymore. But I'd felt different for a little while after all the stuff that had happened with Dahlia this afternoon. And now my parents were ruining it with all their questions. Some part of me knew that they were doing it out of concern. They wanted my life back on track. But I couldn't stand the way they acted with me.

"Sorry, Mom. Her name's Dahlia."

"Would you like to invite her over for dinner sometime? I know you run around all over town,

Stephanie, but it's not really safe."

"Look, Mom, lighten up, will you? What could happen to me, huh? I mean, what more could happen to me?"

"Young lady, I don't appreciate you talking to your mother that way." Young lady? He must have been renting *Leave It to Beaver* on cassette lately. My parents just don't know how to talk to me anymore. "In any case," my father continued, "why don't you invite your friend over for dinner?"

I'm surprised he didn't call her my "little friend" or something like that. Maybe I should have Dahlia meet them. I was sure her forthright way of talking would shock my dad out of his newly acquired sitcom mode. I could just see my parents' faces if she let something like the hooker comment slip over the roast beef. Jesus, they'd think I had a whole new set of problems, all right. I started to laugh.

"I don't know, Dad, maybe I'll ask her sometime. So what's for dinner, anyway?" I started to walk toward the dining room. My mother and father were staring at me.

"What did I do wrong now?" I asked. "Should I have asked permission to leave the room or something?"

"No," my father said.

I looked at my mother. She shook her head slowly.

"That's just the first time we've heard you laugh in months," she said.

I paused at the entrance to the dining room.

She was right.

CHAPTER SIX

Wednesday afternoon I got uptown about half an hour early for my session with Dr. Steinhart. I didn't feel like reading any of the six-year-old magazines hanging around the waiting room, so I decided to get a cup of coffee. His office wasn't too far from a coffee shop I used to go to. It was near a TV studio, and I used to wait there in between auditions.

I sat down in one of the booths in the back and tried to get the waitress's attention. I guess she couldn't see me. I was about to move when I decided that anonymity might be a good thing after all, as a bunch of actors I used to know trooped in. Great, just what I didn't need. I hoped they wouldn't see me. I didn't know them from acting class, just from auditions and stuff, so it wouldn't be like it was with Claudia. Still, I hated running into anyone from my old life. I knew if they saw me they'd ask why they hadn't seen me on the audition circuit lately, and I wanted to be spared the nightmare of that conversation. I hid my face behind the menu, but I couldn't stop myself from listening to them.

"Five BLTs and Diet Cokes to go," one of them ordered. Then the whole group sat down to wait.

"So get this," one of the girls said. I wasn't sure I remembered her name. Janie or something. "I go to this audition for some Tampax commercial. I do really well, get a couple of callbacks. They're talking with my agent, discussing money, everything looks hunky-dory. All of a sudden everything's shot. So my agent calls— what's the deal, you know? And the director tells him my boobs are too small for anyone to believe I have my period yet!"

"Have you thought about silicone?" one of the guys said. Him I definitely remembered. His name was Ethan.

"Have you thought about a nose job?"

"Well, no one's giving me shit about my looks."

I'd had conversations like this a million times. It was the kind of bitchy actor talk that made me glad I wasn't in the business anymore. They sounded so wrapped up in their own stupid problems, like nothing else mattered except whether they booked a commercial or not. I remember Laurie used to have her dermatologist's beeper number in case she got a zit the night before an audition! Did I used to be that bad?

Maybe I still was. After all, I was all wrapped up in my own little world. Still, what I was going through was a hell of a lot more important than whether I looked busty enough for a Tampax ad. Listening to them made me really embarrassed about how petty actors are. As much as I could live without it, though, it made me feel kind of homesick. Homesick for a state of mind. I remember when I used to look as confidant as they did, as if nothing could touch me. I looked over at myself in the mirror near the booth I was sitting in. These days I looked sort of lost.

"Hey, hey, I know you, you're, give me a sec, what's your name?" I whipped my head around. Ethan was staring at me.

"I, uh, I don't think . . ."

"Sorry, I thought I recognized you, you look sort of like this girl I used to know. I only saw your profile before, but now I can tell you're not her. She was really . . ." He trailed off, embarrassed. He wasn't half as uncomfortable as I was, though. I didn't know whether to be relieved that he thought he'd made a mistake, or miserable that I looked so different now. What was he going to say? That I had been really pretty? Really thin?

"Sorry," I said. "It must have been somebody else." But he'd already lost interest, and had gone back to arguing with Janie. I was just wondering how I could leave. I didn't want to stick around near them anymore, when the waitress called out that their order was ready. I kept sitting even after they left. It was time for my session but I kind of felt paralyzed. I could see in the mirror why he thought I was someone else. "Sort of lost" was a nice way of putting it. I looked like I'd been to hell and back, which I suppose, considering my time at Pleasantville, was a pretty apt description. I pulled my hair out of the ponytail I wore every day now, and shook it loose. There. That was a little better, wasn't it? Maybe I should really work and lose the weight I'd put on. But in my heart I knew that it wasn't the hair, or the pounds, that had made Ethan think that I was someone else. It was my whole aura. No matter what I did with my hair or my body, I looked dirty, as if the whole world could see my shameful little secret. I saw in the mirror that a tear was making its way down my cheek. I pulled some napkins from the dispenser. I had to stop crying all the time. Lately I felt like I had a permanent case of PMS. I realized that I was late for my appointment.

"You're late," Dr. Steinhart said when I finally showed up.

"Sorry," I mumbled.

"Any special reason?"

What did he have, radar? I knew from Dr. Marks

that being late was considered a sign of "resistance," but still, why couldn't Rob just assume I'd gotten stuck in the subway?

"Stephanie?" he persisted.

I could tell from the tone in his voice that he wasn't going to let this one drop so easily. "Okay, all right, I kinda had a hard time at some coffee shop. Are you happy?"

"What do you mean, 'hard time'?"

"I don't know. I ran into some actors I used to know, that's all."

"And it wasn't a pleasant experience?"

Sometimes the way he talks kills me. I mean really, "a pleasant experience"? He made it sound like a tea party. "You're really swift, you know that?" I said with more than a touch of bitterness. "From what I've told you, do you think it would be a 'pleasant experience'?"

"Stephanie, as I reminded you last time, you really haven't told me anything about your acting experiences. I know that you used to be in commercials, that you stopped because of your emotional problems, and that you studied some kind of acting technique called 'sense memory.'"

Sense memory. Yeah, I'd mentioned it to him, but no more than that.

"Well, I wasn't upset because of any sense memory

today, okay? I just didn't like seeing them. They didn't even recognize me! They couldn't even tell that I was the same girl!"

Dr. Steinhart perked up. "Stephanie, you just said that you weren't upset by any sense memory today—were you implying that that's usually the reason you're upset? Is there anything you can tell me about that?"

Does sense memory usually upset me? Well, no, not more than having a nervous breakdown.

"Okay, Stephanie, don't give me any bullshit. Let's go." It was Jim's voice I was hearing, not Dr. Steinhart's. Jim's voice in my head.

"But Jim, I don't know what you want."

"Listen, kiddo, don't I always tell you that all good things come to those who wait? Just give me a chance to explain. Jesus." He looked around the room at everyone. "There's one in every class. Look, Stephanie, I tell someone else they're ready for the affective memory, they'd be creaming. It's like the graduate level of sense memory, but you, you've gotta question me."

"Okay, Jim," I said. "So what is it you want me to do?"

"Okay, the affective memory is a personal exercise. It's not like the sunshine or the shower, or any of the basic exercises. You pick a memory," he paused, "a significant memory, and you put yourself back into that state, you see what comes up."

"You mean you kind of hypnotize yourself?"

"Don't make it sound so mystical. It's more like you make yourself emotionally available for the old feelings to come up."

I must have looked baffled, as usual.

"Look, when I was learning, the memory I picked was hearing my grandfather had died. I remembered where I was when I got the news. You get yourself relaxed with your circle of attention complete. Then you pick descriptive words to help access the state."

"Huh?"

"C'mon, Stephanie, you've been doing this long enough, you should have some idea of what I mean."

"I'm sorry, Jim. I don't."

"All right, when I heard about my grandfather I was doing summer stock in Maine. It was spring. I was on the porch of the house where I was renting a room. I remember the smell of the lilacs, the way the white paint was flaking off the clapboard, things like that. So when I want to do an affective memory, I say things like *porch swing, white paint*, and all the stuff comes up. You got it?"

"I got it. What memory should I pick?"

"Jesus, like I know your whole life story?

Anything bad ever happen to you, your grandparents die?"

I shook my head.

"Yeah, well, Miss Charmed Life, something must have happened. You break a leg or an arm?"

I thought for a few minutes. "Well, I got this really bad burn once, from the radiator in the bathroom. No one could figure out how I got it, either, because my nanny was with me."

Jim rolled his eyes. "A nanny yet. I wasn't kidding when I said 'charmed life.' All right, a burn, it'll have to do."

I nodded.

"So, you got this burn in your bathroom. Okay, what color were your bathroom tiles? White?"

"White and blue."

"Fine, you say 'blue and white tiles, peach towels,' whatever the hell color scheme your mom used. Or the decorator. Christ, a nanny . . ."

Phew, I was glad we got that settled. I was afraid that I wouldn't be able to pick a memory.

"Oh, Stephanie?"

"Yeah?"

"One more thing, you'll do it in front of everybody."

"Excuse me?"

"The affective memory, the class watches you. Don't worry, baby, you're gonna dazzle us."

Well, I sure had dazzled them with it. But not in the way anyone expected. At least now I knew how I'd gotten the burn.

"Stephanie."

I looked up. This time it was Dr. Steinhart speaking. Judging from the look on his face I must really have been gone. He seemed pretty concerned.

"You want to tell me what just happened? Where you just were?"

Tell him? Uh-uh, no way, besides . . . "Time's up," I said, and closed his office door.

CHAPTER SEVEN

"By the way," said Mr. Friedman as he handed back the *Rebecca* quizzes, "have any of you opened the book? Only a couple of you did well, and more than a couple of you failed."

I grabbed mine as he handed it to me so no one else could see it, but I didn't have to worry. I'd gotten an A. I turned to look at Dahlia. She grinned at me, then flashed me her quiz. She'd gotten an A too.

I returned her smile tiredly. I'd hardly gotten any sleep the night before. I was afraid that if I closed my eyes I'd see more of the same stuff that had come up in my session, and that was the last thing I wanted. For the first time in ages, it felt good to be in school. After the episode in Dr. Steinhart's office, it was a relief to have to be thinking about stuff like irregular verbs. The only problem was that school would be over soon, and then I'd be left alone in my head again. I knew that my parents were going out that night, and the only thing worse than arguing with them would be staying home by myself. I used to love being by myself. That's part of why I never really missed having friends that much. At least I had one compensation to make up for how I'd changed in the past year. Dahlia. We'd become even closer since I'd shown her my tapes. And I knew that even though I felt pretty useless most of the time, she really appreciated my listening to her problems too. It meant a lot to me that she knew about what had once been the most important part of my life. It's funny, even though it made me happy to tell her part of my story, I knew it would ruin things between us if I let her in on the rest. I mean, when you consider how my parents had changed toward me, imagine what it would do to a friend. And let's just say by some miracle she didn't change toward me, I would still be too ashamed to tell her. Anyway, maybe Dahlia would want to go to a movie with me tonight, maybe we could get together and get our homework done in time for the eight o'clock show. Her mother really liked me now, and I figured that as long as we didn't have any schoolwork she'd be okay with letting Dahlia off the hook for the night. The theater that I liked was showing a Cary Grant series. *Notorious* was playing. I was sure that if Dahlia had liked Olivier, she'd love Cary Grant, and it would definitely keep my mind off things.

"Listen, do you want to go and see another old

movie?" I asked her when the bell rang.

"You should have asked me before. I'm meeting Daryll tonight. My mom's working overtime all week getting some brief done for her boss, otherwise she'd kill me. Hey, are you all right?"

"Yeah, I'm fine." I supposed I could always go by myself, but it wasn't the same.

"Look, you seem pretty down. I'd cancel with Daryll, except he's leaving for South Carolina soon."

"No, really, Dahlia, it's okay. I'll talk to you tomorrow." I didn't want her to feel sorry for me or anything. I guessed I'd just have to make the best of things.

"I'm in my bedroom, Steph," my mom called when I got home.

"Where's Dad?" I wandered into her room. I sat down on the floor and watched her put on her makeup. *Boy, I really must be lonely tonight*, I thought. Sitting in my mother's dressing room watching her get ready was a thing of the past. I hadn't done anything like this with my mom in almost a year.

"He's with some clients. I'm meeting him at the restaurant."

"Oh." Because of my father's job in advertising, he and my mom always got to go to these really fancy restaurants to entertain the agency's clients.

"That looks really good, Mom." She was sitting in front of her dressing table putting her hair up in a French twist.

My mother looked shocked for a second. Was I so nasty to her that it was such a surprise when I was nice? "Thanks, honey," she recovered. "What color lipstick do you think I should wear with my outfit?" I knew my mom knew exactly what color she was going to wear. In fact she already had her makeup on. But I knew also that she didn't want to break the mood. She was probably thinking of the way we used to get along. It had been a pretty standard thing for me to help her get ready in the past. After eleven years of TV commercials, what I didn't know about makeup wasn't worth knowing. I looked at the dress, a champagne-colored silk. "Ugh, wipe off that red, you need a soft color, peach or something."

My mother dutifully wiped off her lipstick, which had in fact looked fine. But I had felt like playing along with her too, as if things were like they'd always been. I couldn't feel the way I once did with her, but I wished that I did. Being with her now, like this, was really bittersweet. It made me wish that things were the way they used to be, before last year. Back then we'd all been ignorant. None of us knew the time bomb that I'd been sitting on. Good old sense memory.

"Okay, that about does it." My mother finished getting dressed and slipped on her coat. "Are you sure you'll be all right alone?" Her forehead puckered in her now familiar frown. Her sudden overprotectiveness irritated me. Never mind the fact that I'd been wondering the same thing for the past couple of hours, why didn't she have more faith in me? Why couldn't she just assume that I'd be okay?

"I'll be fine, Mom," I said shortly. The closeness of the moment before evaporated as suddenly as if it had never been there.

"I left you some money on the table so you could order in Chinese. Have a good night, sweetie." My mother leaned over to kiss me, but I turned my face away.

I had a lot of homework to do, but I turned the stereo on extra loud. Not acid rock or anything, or the neighbors would complain. I put on some Mozart, and then put a tape in the VCR. I didn't even look to see which one it was. After all, I was going to do my homework. I just wanted a lot of sound in the apartment, to drown out my own thoughts. It was actually a pretty effective technique, I realized, when I looked up from my books for the first time in two hours. I'd gotten a lot of stuff done, and by then I was starving. I ordered in, and was working my way through some spareribs when the phone rang.

"Hello?"

"You always answer the phone with your mouth full?"

"Dahlia!" I swallowed my food.

"Do your parents have some wild party going on or something?"

"Not quite, hold on a sec." I put the phone down and went to turn off the stereo and TV.

"Listen, girl, I gotta see you."

"I thought you were with Daryll."

"Yeah, well, there's been a change of plans."

"Where are you?"

"Near that movie theater you like."

"Oh, great! I haven't seen *Notorious* in ages. It's my favorite Hitchcock, too—you'll love it!"

"Huh?" Dahlia sounded confused. "Listen, I need to see you, not some movie. There's a Twin Donut on the corner. Can you meet me in twenty minutes?"

"Sure." I hung up the phone. I wondered what had happened between her and Daryll. She hadn't sounded that great. I grabbed my coat and left.

"Dahlia, what's wrong?" She was waiting outside the Twin Donut, and she looked like she'd been crying.

"That asshole and I had an argument."

"C'mon, let's go inside."

"So what happened?" I asked after we had sat down and Dahlia had placed her usual order of two donuts.

"Oh, he's only going to be in town for a few more days before he goes back to South Carolina, and he wanted me to stay out and party with him. I have a quiz in trig tomorrow, though, and I want to do really well in it. I wouldn't even have gone out with him tonight to begin with, except he's only going to be around for another few days. Plus, like I told you, I knew I could get away with it since my mother isn't around."

"Did you tell him about your quiz?" I was surprised that Dahlia would jeopardize something like that. She wasn't above skipping study hall now and then, but she always got her work done.

"I tried to, but he just gave me shit, he started yelling that I was too young for him. He said he doesn't need to go out with some kid who's still doing her homework." She sniffed.

I was silent. I don't have much practice when it comes to giving advice about boyfriend trouble. Daryll didn't sound like such a good bet to me, but what did I know?

"I gotta do something to make him realize he needs me. If he sees how important I am to him, then he won't treat me this way. Whattaya think?"

"Well, don't look at me. I don't have any experience in these things." I wanted to help Dahlia; she'd come through for me a lot, but I honestly didn't know what to tell her.

"Yeah, how come you never had a boyfriend? You're really cute," Dahlia said, momentarily diverted from her own problem.

I didn't answer her. I knew why I didn't have one. Before, I'd never had time for one, what with school and commercials and everything. Now that I had time I didn't think I could handle it emotionally.

"If I could just make him jealous or something," Dahlia said. "I know that would get to him, but what can I do? I don't want to go out with some other guy or anything like that. I've got it!" She snapped her fingers. "The Halloween dance at school. The guys at school are all immature kids compared to Daryll, but it's better than nothing."

"Well, how will that make him jealous? I mean, how will he even know that you're there?"

"Listen, this is what I'll do. The dance is on Saturday night, right?"

"Yeah."

"So, that's my last night with Daryll. We're supposed to have a really hot date. Now, I don't want to miss that, but we usually get together around nine.

The dance starts at eight. That means I could have a whole hour at the dance."

"You're losing me."

"Just wait, okay? I'll tell my mother I'm going to the dance, right? Daryll will come to pick me up at nine, and my mother will tell him that I'm at the school Halloween dance. I know my Daryll—when he runs to the school and sees me slow-dancing with some guy, he'll realize how much he needs me. Now, do you have anything to wear?"

"You want me to go with you?"

"Of course. You'll come, won't you?"

I shrugged my shoulders, embarrassed but pleased. "I've never been to a dance before." I wasn't as sure about Dahlia's plan as she was. I didn't see how doing all this at the dance would have the effect she wanted, but I felt like it was my turn to help her out. "Sure." I nodded.

Dahlia looked relieved. "Thanks, what have you got to wear?"

"What do people usually wear to a dance?"

"Where you been living? I guess I better lend you something. I've got a great leather miniskirt. Do you have cute legs?" She glanced under the table. "You're wearing jeans, I can't even tell. How come you never wear skirts? I mean, you're always wearing such baggy clothes. It's like you don't want anyone to notice your body."

She was right about that one.

"Like that sweatshirt, I can't even tell if you have big boobs or not." She leaned over and looked down the front of my sweatshirt. "Wow, you're like a C cup or something! Why do you go around hiding that?"

"Dahlia!" I shrieked. "Stop that!" More than a few of the sleazier guys in the place had turned to watch us. "This is the way everyone else at school dresses."

Dahlia shook her head. "Not really. It's like you wear the same clothes, but something about you is different. I mean, yeah, everyone hangs out in sweatshirts, but yours are three sizes too big."

"Listen," I said, somewhat exasperated, "you didn't get me to meet you here to discuss my wardrobe did you?"

"Okay, okay, forget it. I'm just saying you should make more use of your natural talents, that's all. I mean, you couldn't have dressed like this when you were doing all that TV stuff, could you? You must have worn fancier stuff then."

"Yeah, but I don't think that any of the things I used to wear to auditions would be right to wear to a dance. And besides, I hope my natural talents are more substantial than just having big breasts."

That sobered her. "That's one of the reasons I love Daryll. I mean, if I was going out with someone our age he'd be in it for the sex. But Daryll is older. He's interested in more than that. I mean, he would love to, you know, but he's willing to wait until I'm ready." She looked at her watch. "I've gotta get out of here. I've got to start memorizing my trig identities. You be careful going home, okay?"

"You too."

"Don't worry, sweetheart, I know how to handle these creeps."

I decided to walk home. It was only about a mile and the streets were crowded.

I couldn't believe I was going to go to the Halloween dance. I wondered if I should tell my parents. It would make them so happy. That was the kind of wholesome activity they were hoping I'd get involved in at my new school. Maybe I would even have some fun, although I didn't know if I'd feel that comfortable dancing with any guys. I was impressed with how easy it was for Dahlia to talk about bodies and relationships and things like that. The most intimate conversations I'd had with girls before had just been about periods and stuff. I didn't think I'd known anyone else who would look down the front of my sweatshirt in public! Even though her behavior shocked me, I couldn't help wishing I was more like her in some ways. One thing was for sure. It would be nice to feel comfortable living in my own body again. Who knows, maybe if I stuck with Dahlia some of her relaxed attitude would rub off on me. *Yeah, right,* I told myself. I should be so lucky.

CHAPTER EIGHT

Saturday morning I woke up early. I was supposed to meet Dahlia around three to go shopping for the dance, then we were going to go back to my apartment to get ready.

It was such a gorgeous day that I didn't feel like hanging around the apartment. I decided to go out and do some window-shopping or walk in the park. Fifth Avenue was really crowded, but I love walking down it and looking in the windows. I went into Saks and looked around for a while, but I didn't see anything that I really liked. I decided to wait until I went shopping with Dahlia. I just hoped that she wouldn't come up with anything too wild or revealing for me to wear.

After wandering around for a couple hours I was pretty hungry. There weren't any cheapo coffee shops in the neighborhood I was in. I was trying to figure out if I should walk back home for lunch when I saw a really cute place.

It was kind of fancy, but not too. The menu in the

window wasn't exactly inexpensive, but it wasn't that bad either. It was the kind of place my agent used to take me to whenever I booked a commercial. I hadn't spent a lot of money on myself lately, since I'd been sticking pretty close to home. Besides, I didn't have the expenses that I used to have either. Getting head shots reprinted costs a fortune, not to mention all the other stuff you need when you're an actress. I figured I deserved to have a nice lunch.

I walked in and sat at one of the overstuffed banquets. The whole place was really pretty, with flowers everywhere.

I ordered some tea and a chicken salad. I felt a little out of place. There wasn't anyone else there dressed as casually as I was.

The waitress plonked down my cup of tea, sloshing some onto the table. I picked up my napkin and started wiping it up. The napkin was blue-and-white flowered, made out of the same material as the drapes. I looked around, the whole place was done in blue and white. Why hadn't I noticed that before?

The tea was hot. I looked down into the cup, and the steam rose and covered my face in a kind of fog. For a second the place around me was obscured by it.

"Okay, are you ready, Stephanie? I don't have time for any bullshit now, let's get going." Jim's voice was even more sarcastic than usual. "So let's see you re-create this burn, okay?"

I sat down in my chair and started to relax. I was pretty deep into it when I heard Jim's voice in my ear.

"Okay, Stephanie, are you relaxed, baby?"

I nodded yes.

"Good, start with the words, and let whatever comes up come up."

It's funny, you'd think that I would feel really self-conscious with everyone watching, but I didn't. It's sort of amazing the way that sense memory works, you get so concentrated that it's almost trancelike. I could imagine getting in so deep that nothing would pull me out.

Time to start the words. I had written down a list of descriptive words at home, stuff that I thought would help bring the memory back. You're supposed to practice a sense memory at home before you bring it into class. But I'd been kind of lazy this past week. I hoped that the words I'd picked would work.

"White and blue tiles . . . yellow towels . . ." Yellow towels, not peach. "Mr. Bubble . . ."

I could hear a couple giggles from the back of the class. Jim made shushing noises.

I definitely felt like I was in my bathroom, and I felt like I was five years old again too. But nothing too

earth-shattering was happening. I started to concentrate on the words associated more with the burn.

"Radiator . . . stool . . ." My nanny used to dry me
off while I was sitting on a stool. What else had I written down?

"Starched white cotton," that was the feel of her
uniform.

All of a sudden, I jumped. I could feel my arm
being burned, and something else too, some other pressure on my arm, what was it?

"Okay, Stephanie, relax into it," I heard Jim's voice
again.

"Come a little closer, that's right, just a little closer."
That wasn't Jim's voice, or my voice either. And the
pressure on my arm, it was almost worse than the
burning sensation I was remembering.

"Yellow towels . . ." I tried to center myself with
the words.

"Come on, now, that's a good girl. Just a little bit
closer now."

"Where? Come where?" I was whimpering.

Jim was at my elbow. "Take it easy, Stephanie,
maybe you want to come out of this now."

But I was too far gone. And the voice in my head,
what did it want? Why did my arm hurt so much?

"Are you going to make me hurt you?"

"Nooo!"

"Okay, Steph, let's end this now!"

But I couldn't hear Jim's voice, not above the other one.

"Come on. It will be our little game. No one has to know. What would you rather have, me or the radia-tor? I'll tell your parents you were a bad girl." She twisted my arm some more.

"I don't want to! I don't want to!"

"Stop! Stephanie, stop! I want you to come out of this right now!" Jim was shouting.

I wanted to come out, but I was crying so hard that I didn't know if I could.

"Please let me go! You're hurting me!" I yelled at my nanny.

She was the voice, she was holding my arm against the radiator because I didn't want to do what she wanted.

"Ooow!"

Slam! Jim slapped me across the face. Hard.

I opened my eyes. Everyone in the class looked ashen. Jim looked terrified.

"Okay, Stephanie, are you with me? I'm going to call a doctor."

"No, don't, I'll get in trouble, she doesn't want anyone to know!" To my adult ears the sound of my five-year-old voice sounded strange.

"Jesus Christ," one of the students said.

"Get her to a fucking shrink, man!"

"My God, what a nightmare, do you think she knew?"

"All right everybody, show's over. Clear out." I never heard Jim sound so angry before. "Stephanie, stay with me, baby, can you talk to me?"

I shook my head no. I could hear everything he was saying, I felt like I was floating in and out of reality. Part of me, the adult me was disenfranchised, watching everything from afar. The five-year-old me couldn't stop crying.

"Listen, Stephanie, I'm going to call your parents. I'm going to get them to come and pick you up, okay?"

"No! I don't want my parents! Nothing happened, I just fell against the radiator, see?" The five-year-old held out her arm. Jim glanced down at the thirteen-year-old burn mark. He looked up at me; the part of me that was still rational could see tears in his eyes.

"I'm going to take you home myself, Stephanie, okay? We'll just go outside and get a cab."

I nodded. I love cab rides. "Do I get to tell the driver where we're going? I know my address by heart."

Jim just shook his head and muttered, "Jesus." He took my arm gently and led me out of the classroom.

"Be careful," I said. "My arm is burned, don't squeeze it too hard."

Jim didn't say anything, just hailed a cab and bundled me into it. He let me tell the driver the address all by myself. It was funny, Jim was acting nicer to me than he had since I'd met him. He was almost like a pal. It was too bad I never saw him again.

My mother answered the door. I don't know what Jim told her. She suggested I take a hot bath while she called the doctor. She couldn't understand why I burst into tears when she said that.

The steam from my cup evaporated. My tea had cooled off. The waitress arrived with my chicken salad.

I threw a twenty-dollar bill on the table and ran out of the restaurant. I ran the thirty blocks home. I didn't stop running until I got to the apartment.

I let myself in and dashed to the bathroom. I leaned over the toilet and threw up until there was nothing left to throw up. It wasn't the food in the restaurant. No, really, I'm sure it was great, and I didn't even touch my chicken salad. It's just that I always threw up when I remembered.

CHAPTER NINE

"Come on, you've gotta help me out, I can't be doing all the work here. So, which one do you like?" Dahlia held up two dresses, each ridiculously low cut.

I shrugged my shoulders. "I don't know, Dahlia, they're both okay, I guess, I don't really care." Well, that was true; this morning's trip down memory lane had left me with little energy for anything else.

"What's wrong with you, girl? I mean, I can understand you not being that interested in the dance, but this is important to me."

"I'm sorry, Dahlia." She was right. Besides, thinking about what to wear to the dance would take my mind off other stuff. "Umm, I guess the black is better, the purple is too harsh for you."

"This isn't for me! I already have what I'm going to wear. This is for you."

"For me!" No way was I going to wear anything like that.

"Well, you can't wear that sweatshirt, for crissakes!"

I decided I better put some real effort into shopping. Otherwise Dahlia would dress me up like the Victoria's Secret catalog.

"All right, all right, but I don't want to wear either of those. Couldn't I just wear my jeans with a different top?"

"Well, I guess that's a start," Dahlia mumbled grudgingly. She hung the dresses back up. "C'mon, let's get out of here, this department is just dresses."

Dahlia dragged me all around Bloomingdale's looking for something for me to wear. It would have been fun if I'd been able to keep my mind on what we were doing, but I couldn't stop thinking about my sense memory flashback that morning. I'd hoped that Dahlia's chatter would block everything else out, but even she wasn't that diverting. I kept remembering the look on my mother's face when Jim brought me home. I don't remember everything from that time—it's all very mixed up in my head. But I remember my parents grilling Jim, and him trying to explain what happened. I think things got pretty heated. I don't know how much I contributed to the conversation, but from what my mother told me later, whatever I'd said, I stayed in my five-year-old mode. The first clear thing I remember is waking up at Pleasantville the next day.

My parents had been pretty frantic and at a complete loss as to what to do. Putting aside what they learned from Jim, it was clear I was in a pretty serious state. They'd called the family doctor, who said it sounded as if I needed to be sedated and put into a facility until I calmed down. Luckily Pleasantville wasn't one of your state-run jobs, or I'd still be there now. It was the kind of place where mixed-up rich kids went, and it had been easy for my parents to get me out when they saw how bad it was.

"What about this?" Dahlia's voice cut through my thoughts. I looked at the top she was showing me. A red imitation-leather bustier.

"I don't think so, Dahlia. I really want something a little tamer."

"What is it with you? I don't understand—if I had a pair of C cups I'd show them off every chance I got."

"I'm just not comfortable dressing that way."

"Did some guy ever try and get too fresh with you or anything?"

"No, not exactly."

"Because all you have to do if something like that ever happens is kick them in the balls, you know what I'm saying?"

Of course, everybody says things like that.

Everybody imagines in their head how they'd react if they were mugged or attacked. Everybody's always ready in their imagination with the Mace or whatever. But things don't always work out the way that you think they will.

"There you go again."

"Huh?"

"Sometimes when I'm talking to you, you just go off in your own little world. I guess I understand now, you know, I mean now that you've told me about your problems last year." Dahlia cleared her throat nervously. "I just want you to know that I really appreciate your helping me out tonight. I know my problems with Daryll aren't as serious as whatever you've been through, but, well, if you ever need anything, or you want to talk about it more . . ." She trailed off.

I couldn't believe it, she was actually blushing. "You've already really helped me, Dahlia," I said sincerely. "You shouldn't judge your problems. Mine aren't any more important. Whatever matters to someone matters. You can't place a value on things like that." I was starting to sound like Dr. Steinhart. That was the kind of thing he would say. I guess some of what went on in my sessions was starting to sink in, because I would never have said anything like that otherwise. "Besides, it makes me happy to help you."

Dahlia started laughing. "All right, I don't want this to get all mushy or anything. Help me find you something to wear, we don't want to miss the stupid dance."

We hunted around for another half an hour before we found a bodysuit we both agreed on. It wasn't too low cut for me, and it was just lacy and sheer enough to satisfy Dahlia.

"This is perfect," she said. "It leaves just enough to the imagination." I paid for the bodysuit, and we grabbed a cab to my apartment.

"Come on," I said. "I better introduce you to my parents."

"Honey, is that you?" My mom poked her head around the corner. She looked a little surprised when she saw Dahlia. Well, that wasn't too hard to understand. It had been a long time since she had seen me with anyone.

"Hi, Mom, this is Dahlia. Dahlia, my mom."

"Dahlia, Stephanie's told me so much about you," my mother responded inevitably.

"Dahlia, great to meet you." My father came into the room.

"Would you like anything to eat?" Mom asked.

They both looked pathetically happy that I'd brought Dahlia home. For once their behavior didn't make me angry, I was glad that seeing me with a friend made them happy. Still, though, I wasn't about to let this turn into a little get-together with my parents grilling Dahlia over milk and cookies.

"We're kind of in a hurry," I said before Dahlia could respond. "We have to get ready for the Halloween dance, okay?" I pushed Dahlia toward my room.

"Nice to meet you," Dahlia called over her shoulder.

I dumped my stuff on the bed and headed for my dressing room.

"You have your own dressing room! This is like something out of a TV show or something!"

I looked around, seeing it through her eyes. This is where I used to get ready for auditions. I hadn't spent much time in it lately. After all, I didn't need a sit-down dressing table with stage lights around it to get ready for school in the morning. I had tons of clothes, all very carefully organized. I must have had an outfit to match every possible audition scenario. Some of them were really pretty, too. Maybe I should start dressing the way I used to.

"You didn't see this last time?"

Dahlia shook her head. "No, we just watched your commercials."

"Well, I'd show you around now, but we don't have that much time. I better start doing your makeup."

I grabbed a towel and draped it around Dahlia's neck. "So I won't spill powder on you," I explained.

I started assembling my cosmetics on the counter. I own about as much stuff as a small drugstore.

"I didn't know that you know about makeup. I figured I was gonna have to teach you. I mean, you never wear makeup—where'd you get all this from?"

"Commercials. You have to wear makeup to go on auditions, and on some low-budget commercials you have to do your own makeup for the camera." I started putting foundation on Dahlia. The reason actresses always look like they have such flawless skin, besides airbrushing and Vaseline on camera lenses, is the way they mix their foundation. Most women buy a bottle of the stuff and slap it on. No makeup artist for film would ever do that. No one has skin that looks anything like the colors that come in a bottle, and makeup artists usually mix three or four different colors until they get the perfect match. I finished with the base and looked at Dahlia. I took out my nail scissors and false eyelashes.

"What are you doing now? False eyelashes? I thought you didn't like the sophisticated look."

"I don't," I said, tilting her head back. I started trimming the lashes with the nail scissors until they weren't that much different from Dahlia's own. They were just what you'd have if you'd been born with perfect long eyelashes, but not so long that they looked fake. I glued them on individually. It's not as hard as it sounds, but it is pretty time-consuming. Then I opened a bottle of Liquid Roses, which is this lip dye that's been a Hollywood staple since the forties. Paint it on and it lasts about five hours. The color's good on everyone. It just looks natural, only ten times better. When I finished, Dahlia looked like she had flawless skin and doe eyes, with perfect rosy lips, but not like she was wearing any makeup. I started to fix her hair.

"What if this doesn't work?" Dahlia asked.

"The makeup? You mean what if it doesn't look good?"

"No, I mean what if Daryll doesn't show up? I mean what if when my mother tells him I went to the Halloween dance, he just decides to forget about me?" Dahlia fretted.

"I told you, I don't know anything about this kind of thing, but it seems like you have everything all worked out."

"Yeah, I guess." Dahlia still looked worried. I finished with her hair, which I'd done kind of Scarlett

O'Hara—like, and turned her to look in the mirror.

"What do you think?" I asked.

"It's unbelievable! I've never looked like this! How did you do it! You could be a makeup artist! Shit, when Daryll sees me looking this good he'll go crazy! I look like I could be on TV!"

"You should see what most actresses look like without their makeup," I said. "People think it's a glamorous profession, but you wouldn't think so if you could hang out on a set at five A.M. If you think I did a good job on you just now, you wouldn't believe how a top makeup artist could make you look." I started to put my own makeup on. It was strange to be doing it, as if I were getting ready for an audition again. It took me a lot less time to fix myself up than it did Dahlia. I finished, and we both got dressed. I put on the bodysuit with my jeans, and Dahlia wore a really beautiful purple crushed velvet dress that she had made herself. "Part of the reason I decided to wear this," she said, pulling it out of her backpack, "is that it never looks wrinkled."

"Let's have a look at you two," my father called from the living room. He sounded like he was in one of his bluff and hearty moods. But I figured I could indulge my parents just this once, so Dahlia and I went into the living room to show ourselves off.

"You two look terrific," my mother said, but I could tell she was surprised at my bodysuit.

"Let's take another cab, okay?" Dahlia asked on the way to the elevator. "I can't deal with the subway in high heels."

Pete made a big deal out of getting us a cab when we got downstairs. He always used to tell me how pretty I was when I went out on auditions. He seemed really happy now to see me looking something like my old self again. It reminded me of my run-in with Ethan earlier, and how differently I came across these days.

The dance was already crowded when we got there. Some of the kids had come in Halloween costume, but most people were wearing regular clothes. I noticed that some of the guys in my English class were checking me out in a way that they never had before. It was kind of flattering, but it also embarrassed me. I wasn't sure that if anyone asked me to dance that I would. After all, I kept telling myself that I was just there to lend Dahlia moral support. Of course, Dahlia didn't have any qualms. She was there to make Daryll jealous, and she started dancing with the first guy who asked her. I stood around and held a Coke, trying to look like I was really happy to be there. The music was loud and frantic, and I wondered if Dahlia would even get a chance to slow-dance with some guy like she had planned. I was getting a little tired of pasting a smile on my face.

"Stephanie?"

I turned. Some guy from my French class was smiling at me.

"I'm Tim, I sit two rows behind you, would you like to dance?" A slow dance had just started.

I wanted to say no, but I didn't want to hurt his feelings. Maybe I could use this like a test, and see if it made me sick to be touched by him. I was thinking this over when I noticed what he was wearing. He was one of the people who'd come in costume. He looked like, well, he looked like . . .

"Who are you supposed to be dressed like?"

Tim looked sort of embarrassed. "Oh this, I just sort of raided my father's closet. I think it's more fun to wear a costume on Halloween."

"But who are you?" I persisted. He was wearing black pants tucked into riding boots with a billowy white shirt, and old-fashioned black tails.

"I guess it didn't really work, because nobody in my English class has been able to figure it out. I'm in a different class from you," he added unnecessarily. "And we're reading—"

"*Wuthering Heights*," I said.

"How'd you know?" Tim laughed.

"You look like Heathcliff," I answered. I know that Dahlia would say that he was just a kid, but I thought he looked wonderful.

Tim laughed again. "You're the first person who's gotten it! That's a sign, it means we were meant to dance together."

I'm sure that Dahlia would also find that line really silly, but it didn't bother me. I wondered what it would be like to dance with him, I wondered if I could actually let myself be held in his arms like you do in a slow dance. If I could do that maybe the nightmare of the past year would start to fade.

He put his hand on my arm to lead me out to the dance floor. I know I've said that my father hadn't hugged me in the past year. That was true. Part of it was that he felt uncomfortable around me, but the rest of it was me. I knew that I sent out strong "don't touch me" signals. It's funny, you don't realize how much casual physical contact you have with people until you cut it all off.

A million feelings rushed through me. I felt scared and uncomfortable. All the dirty shameful feelings I had had in the past year rushed to the surface. But in some ways it felt nice, too. He had a light, friendly touch. I looked down at Tim's hand on my arm. He was holding me just below the elbow, a few inches from my burn scar. I jerked my arm away, feeling ashamed and dirty.

Tim looked confused and slightly hurt, and I wondered what I should tell him. It was obvious that we both felt uncomfortable. And to think that for one crazy moment, I was letting myself imagine what it would feel like to be kissed by Heathcliff. "That kind of thing is for other people, Stephanie," I told myself. I had a bad feeling I was going to start crying any second. I was thinking of what I could say and how I could get out of there, when I saw Daryll enter the gym. Dahlia was slow-dancing with some guy. It looked like it was going to go exactly like she planned, except judging from the expression on Daryll's face it didn't seem like the plan had been such a good idea after all.

"Tim, look, I'm sorry. I just saw that a friend of mine's in trouble. I've got to go." I stumbled over the words. I'm sure that they didn't make any sense to Tim, but to save face he pretended like they did.

"Sure, see you around, Stephanie."

I looked over toward Dahlia, and saw that Daryll was already by her side. Dahlia looked thrilled for one second, then she started to cry. It was clear he was shouting at her, but the music was so loud I couldn't hear what was going on. I started making my way toward them through the crush of people. Before I could get there Daryll turned on his heel and left the dance floor.

"Dahlia, what happened?" I could barely hear myself. Dahlia didn't answer, she was crying. "Come on, let's go to the girl's room. It will be quiet there. We can talk." I led Dahlia off the dance floor.

"Oh, Stephanie," she sobbed when we were in the bathroom, "it all backfired! I made him too jealous! He said that if hanging out with guys my own age was more important to me than spending time with him, then he'd break up with me!"

"Couldn't you explain?" I asked.

"You saw what happened out there. He's gone, I know I won't be able to find him tonight, and he leaves for his base at six tomorrow morning. Oh, Stephanie, what am I going to do?" She looked at me, but she was so wrapped up in her own misery that she didn't see the tears that were running down my face in silent imitation of hers.

CHAPTER TEN

Monday afternoon I wasn't sure if I was going to go to Dr. Steinhart's or not. I'd never skipped a session before, though, not with him or any of my other shrinks. It wasn't because I was so committed to therapy. Hardly. It was more that I didn't have anything else to do. But I was getting kind of wary of Dr. Steinhart. Even though I'd barely told him anything, I'd been more open with him than I had been with anyone else. And as far as I was concerned, it wasn't doing me any good. Wasn't it better to keep pushing things down like I had been? It seemed to me that the best way to get over things was not to think about them, and being in therapy three times a week made me think about things a lot. Would I have had that episode in the restaurant if I wasn't seeing a shrink? I knew what Dr. Steinhart would say, he'd say that I was having these things because I *was* pushing them down, because I hadn't "dealt" with them in the sessions. I knew that he was trying to get me to open up more, and I was afraid he might succeed. Maybe it would make more sense if I wanted to talk about it and get it out in the open. But I didn't feel like I could. Something held me back every time. According to the shrink magazines I read in Rob's waiting room, that wasn't so uncommon. He'd even written an article about it himself: "Resistance in the patient-therapist relationship." I'd read every word wondering if each time he described a particularly recalcitrant patient he'd been referring to me. According to the article some people took years before they got going. I didn't intend to be in therapy that long. But still, I just didn't feel ready to dig really deep. There were times, though, that Rob seemed like he really cared, and that made me want to tell him some of the big stuff. I didn't know if he really liked me or anything, but that's the feeling I got from him. Occasionally when I got there early I'd see the patients he had before me on their way out. Most of them looked like society matrons whose biggest problems were where to get a good manicure. I suppose after them I seemed refreshing, or maybe even something of a mystery. So Dr. Steinhart had me wavering about whether to open up more or not, and that wasn't a good thing. You can always talk, but once you've said stuff you can't take it back. I'd tell Dr. Steinhart when I was sure I wanted to, rather than spill the beans prematurely.

If Dahlia had been in any kind of mood to cut study hall and do something, I probably wouldn't have gone. But she was pretty subdued after Saturday night, and just shook her head "no" when I asked her if she wanted to do anything. The idea of skipping my session just to hang out on my own wasn't very appealing, so at three-thirty I found myself on the uptown subway headed toward Dr. Steinhart's office.

Dr. Steinhart didn't seem in the mood to play the staring game. Instead he started right in. I guess my zoning out last week had clued him in that things were happening with me.

"Last session it seemed like something came up. Are you ready to talk about it?"

I was right, he was expecting something. But I was tongue-tied. I should have skipped my session. Maybe I could try and get us back to the staring game. In any case, I could give it my best shot. I gave him a long stare, but he was impervious.

"All right, Stephanie, I'm going to start the ball rolling, so to speak. I know it's hard for you to talk about things of your own accord, but will you answer what I ask you?"

I nodded. That didn't sound too bad. How deep could his questions go?

"I noticed that what seemed to set you off last week was my mentioning sense memory. Can you tell me more about that?"

Maybe I underestimated him. "It's not the easiest thing in the world to talk about," I said. It seemed like he was on the right track after all.

"I can understand that, Stephanie. Being in therapy isn't always a smooth process. That's why I've done a little research on my own, to help move things forward."

"Research?"

For answer Dr. Steinhart held up *Method or Madness*, the sense memory method bible. "It's not hard to see that you're very sensitive regarding your acting training. I thought I'd read up on it, and that we could use it as a jumping-off point."

Jumping off what? Cliffs? But still, I was impressed, and kind of touched, too. I mean, Dr. Stevenson would never have done anything like this. She forgot about me the minute I walked out the door. Maybe I was right about Rob; maybe he did care.

"To be honest, I didn't know what to expect when I started reading, but this sense memory technique is quite fascinating. I'm not qualified to rate it as an acting technique, but it seems like it has very important psychological implications. This whole idea of being able to access any emotional state at will is fraught with possibilities, both exciting and worrisome. To put it another way, this sense memory really seems like a loaded gun."

That was for sure.

"I can understand how those skills would be invaluable to a performer; at the same time, if one was emotionally vulnerable to begin with, then I think the technique could be somewhat dangerous."

"Did my parents tell you anything?"

"Stephanie, you know how therapy works, complete confidentiality. I couldn't have talked to your parents without your knowing."

I nodded, relieved; it had almost seemed like he knew everything.

"Stephanie, I feel like there's something brewing here, right under the surface. I'd like to help you, but you're going to have to help me. Was there anything in particular about the sense memory that you feel contributed to your breakdown?"

"Well, I . . ." Now was the time to tell him, but I couldn't somehow. It was so much easier not to deal with this stuff. Couldn't we play the staring game? I would even have taken a number twelve expression.

"Okay, Stephanie, I'm going to fish." He opened the

book. "Let's see, did you ever do an exercise called 'morning drink'?"

I smiled. "Everyone does that. It's the first exercise; it's how you train your imagination for the stuff to come."

"Doesn't sound like a problem." He looked at me questioningly.

"Uh-uh, it wasn't. It's pretty neat, actually. I mean training your imagination, creating a cup of coffee that doesn't exist. You start off with your strongest sense— some people have a really great sense of smell, for instance. So okay, you close your eyes and try and get the smell of your coffee. At first when you're doing it you just think it's ridiculous, but all of a sudden, wham! You smell hazelnut blend or whatever. Then you try and get the feel of the cup—is it china, or some paper deal from a diner? Maybe that sounds stupid, but it's amazing. You wouldn't believe how easy it is to start really feeling all this stuff. Maybe you think being able to smell some nonexistent coffee isn't that important, but it's how you start believing other things, like that you're really the prince of Denmark." Rob looked interested, but maybe he was just relieved that I was talking.

"Okay, so that wasn't any trouble for you. How about the next exercise—'taste'?"

"That's pretty easy. You just pick a distinctive taste and focus on that. Most people pick a lemon."

"What about 'smell'?"

"That's pretty easy too. Everybody thinks nothing will happen with that one, but it's pretty . . . evocative. I picked my nursery school teacher's perfume. But there was this older woman in my class who picked the smell of this weird malt drink she used to have as a kid in England. Anyway, she was just doing her work, trying to re-create the smell, when she went wild. It turned out that the last time she'd drunk it had been as a child during World War Two, and it brought up all these memories of being in the Blitz."

Rob looked quite interested about that one. "It doesn't surprise me that someone could have a reaction like that. Psychiatrists have known for a long time that the sense of smell is a powerful trigger. What concerns me is how uncontrolled this process seems. It's not always beneficial to have feelings come up that one isn't prepared for. Did something like that happen to you, Stephanie?"

"Why do you ask?" I tried to act like he hadn't said anything important, but even Olivier couldn't have carried that off.

Rob just gave me a look. Not number twelve, but not number five either. He looked like he knew I was hiding something. He went back to the book in his hand.

"How about the rest of these?" He rattled off the exercises. "'Place, sound, hot, cold, mirror, sunshine, private moment'? How did you do with those?"

"They weren't any problem."

"Well, if you did all of those, then you must have done all the basic sensory exercises."

"Sure."

"Well, that only leaves the affective memory."

Bingo.

"Can you tell me about that? The book isn't too clear."

Yeah right, bullshit, as if I could explain it any better than the book. I should have seen it coming, he'd been leading me on the whole time. "You're pretty sneaky, you know that?" I said angrily. "How do you know anything happened?"

"I don't know, Stephanie, I can only guess, and after talking to you and reading the book I was able to make an educated guess."

"Yeah, well, Mr. Educated Guesser, you can just figure out the rest!" I started to cry.

"Stephanie, please understand, my goal is to help you, that's why I'm doing this. Help me help you. Tell me about your affective memory. What memory did you choose? Why did you choose something if you knew it would upset you so much? Did you think it would be more dramatic?"

"I didn't know it would upset me!" I yelled. "I didn't know. You're supposed to pick a significant memory, like your grandparents dying or something. I picked getting this burn, see? That was the only thing I could think of to pick. My acting teacher made fun of me, he said I'd had a charmed life, a lot he knew!" I shoved my arm in front of his face. "That's all I thought I was doing, picking the memory of the burn, but it wasn't that simple."

"What happened?" Dr. Steinhart asked.

"Well, you read the book, you know how it works. I thought of the circumstances surrounding the burn, you know, like you're supposed to." I hoped he could understand what I was saying, I was crying pretty hard. "I picked words that would describe the situation as I remembered it. All of a sudden I started remembering other things, things I'd blocked out for over ten years!"

"What things, Stephanie?"

I squirmed with embarrassment.

"What things, Stephanie?" Dr. Steinhart repeated.

"I—I wasn't alone when I got burned. I had a nanny, she was with me."

"And?"

"Stop asking me questions! You're so good at figuring things out, you figure that one out! You know what she did!" I shouted. "It was because of her I got the burn! Because she forced me, she made me do things, she . . ."

"Okay, Stephanie, calm down. Clearly we need to go into this further, but we only have a few minutes left, and it's not a good idea to dig too deep when we don't have enough time to fully explore. I'd just like to leave you with a few thoughts that you can mull over before our next appointment. First of all, I'm curious, did you go into this with any of your other therapists?"

"No," I choked out. I was relieved that there were only a couple minutes left. I felt wiped out.

"And is this the reason that you were uncomfortable seeing female therapists?"

"I guess so."

"All right. It's important for you to realize that whatever happened to you, you survived it. Somebody did something horrible to you, that can't be undone, but you can work through it in here. You can come to terms with it and move on. I know that sounds like cold comfort now, Stephanie, but I've had other patients who've had similar experiences. They're able to work through them, though, and believe it or not, they're often stronger for it. You made an important start here today."

I nodded as I gathered my things and left the office, but I wasn't really listening too carefully. He could talk all he wanted to, but what did he know? Dr. Steinhart may have been a shrink for twenty-five years, but he'd never been through what I had. How did he know that things would get better? He couldn't imagine how dirty I felt all the time. He thought I'd be able to "work through things." Get everything all tidied up inside.

But I knew I'd never be clean.

CHAPTER ELEVEN

"Hey, are you running off to your head doctor, or what?" Dahlia asked. It was Wednesday after English class, and we hadn't talked that much since the scene with Daryll on Saturday night.

"Not today, my shrink canceled." Dr. Steinhart had called me before I left for school. He had a fever and was taking the day off. He told me how sorry he was to be putting things on hold after such a "productive" session, and that he would see me Friday. I didn't mind the interruption: I needed a break. "How come? Are you feeling okay?" She looked pretty depressed, actually.

"You feel like missing study hall for a change?"

I wondered what she had in mind. Nobody expected me in study hall anyway. "Sure, what's up?"

"Let's go get something to eat, okay? I really want to talk to you." She looked relieved.

"Any place special?"

"I can't think. You pick someplace."

I didn't feel like spending a lot of money, and I was in the mood for junk food, so I picked a diner near school. Dahlia didn't seem to care one way or the other and barely even glanced at the menu. She could hardly even stand to wait while the guy took my order.

"Okay, listen, I've got an idea," Dahlia announced as soon as the waiter had left.

"An idea? About what?" I couldn't figure out what she meant.

"About Daryll, how to get him back."

"Oh no, wait a minute. Your last idea didn't exactly work out. Don't you think you should just leave well enough alone?"

Dahlia looked hurt. "What am I supposed to do? Forget about him? I love him, I've got to get him back."

I studied her face. She looked as miserable as I'd been feeling lately. Maybe she was right, maybe she did need to get him back. I felt bad that she seemed so depressed. I almost felt like I was dragging her down to my level. If trying to get him back would cheer her up, I should at least listen. "Okay, shoot. What's the idea?"

She seemed kind of nervous all of a sudden. I was surprised. Dahlia was usually so forthright. "Well, the thing is, I need your help."

Why would asking that make Dahlia uneasy? I wondered. "Okay, no problem, what is it?"

"Well, I mean it's a pretty big deal." Now she looked really uncomfortable.

"Come on, tell me! Get to the point already!"

Dahlia took a deep breath. "All right, the thing is I need to borrow some money, and, well, I need you, too."

"Dahlia, you're driving me crazy! Money's no problem, unless you want to borrow five thousand dollars, and you know you can count on me. But what is it? What's your idea?" There had to be something else. I knew Dahlia was uncomfortable about asking for the loan, but that didn't explain the expression she had on her face.

"The last time I saw Daryll was on Saturday night." She paused.

"Yeah, so?"

"After he ran off he didn't go home all night, or if he did, he didn't answer his phone. I must have called him about a thousand times."

"Go on."

"Okay, so the next morning he left for his base, right?"

"Right." I wished she'd hurry up with this.

"I know he's at the base. I mean, he'd be court-martialed or something if he hadn't shown up, but he won't take my phone calls."

"What do you mean he 'won't take' your phone calls? Who answers the phone, anyway?"

"Man, you don't know anything about being a Marine, do you? It's not like he's one of these Wall Street types walking around with a cellular phone! If I want to talk to him I gotta call the head honcho's office, and they're only allowed to accept personal phone calls at certain times. He must have told them he was forfeiting his personal calls or something."

"Maybe you should write to him."

"What do you think, girl? I've been sending letters twice a day. But if he won't come to the phone when I call, how do I know he'll even open my letters?"

I guess she wanted to borrow some money to send a telegram or something. After all, the one thing I knew about telegrams was that you had to sign for them personally. But why was she being so skittish about asking? It was no big deal.

"So, if I can't talk to him, and writing to him is pointless," Dahlia went on, "I figure there's only one thing left for me to do."

"Let me guess, you want to send him a telegram, right?"

"A telegram? What's with you? Are you crazy?

What good would a telegram do? What could I even say in a telegram? 'I love you, stop. I'm sorry, stop'?"

"Okay, okay, I guess it's a stupid idea. So what's your plan, then?"

"Listen, we have a three-day weekend coming up, right?"

"Yeah," I answered. Next Monday was some school holiday.

"So I want to go down to his base and visit him. It's an overnight bus trip, but if you leave Friday night the bus gets in just in time for visiting hours on Saturday. Sunday the bus leaves at eight P.M., and doesn't get back until Monday morning. But that's cool, 'cause there are no classes Monday."

"I don't believe you!"

"Why not? I called Greyhound."

"Not about the bus schedule! I mean that you're even thinking of doing this!"

"There's nothing else I can do. Really, I'm going crazy. I've got to straighten this out with him."

"Couldn't you at least try a telegram, or a fax, or something?"

"Stephanie! Listen to me here! I'm falling apart!"

That stopped me. If there was anything that would really make me listen to her it was those words. No one understood them better than I did. I didn't think she was just being melodramatic, either. I'd never seen her look this bad before. I didn't know what to do. I really wanted to help Dahlia. It was painful to see her this unhappy. But I didn't know how to help her. Would it be better to lend her the money or to try and talk her out of it? I decided that the whole thing was too crazy to go along with.

"Look, Dahlia, I really want to help you, it's just that I think this is a really bad idea. How do you know he'll even see you? If he won't answer your phone calls, and you're sure that he's not reading your letters, it doesn't sound like he'll welcome you with open arms." That made sense. She'd have to see the logic behind that.

Dahlia just smiled. "Oh, I know my Daryll. When he realizes how serious I am about getting back together with him, he'll see me."

"You know him? Like you knew that making him jealous with the Halloween dance was a good idea?"

Dahlia's face crumpled. I felt bad that I'd hurt her.

"Yeah, okay, so I made a mistake. But I know this is going to work. Besides, nothing you can say will stop me. I'm going to do it."

She sounded pretty determined. I wondered if I should tell her mother, but she'd never forgive me. But never mind *me* telling her mother, how was *Dahlia* going to tell her? Wasn't her mother going to notice if Dahlia wasn't around for the weekend? I knew her mother was pretty strict about things like homework, and I didn't imagine that something like this would go over too well. Maybe when Dahlia thought about that part she'd back down. "How are you going to get this by your mother, huh? I mean, Dahlia, she gets upset if you're out late on a school night. You want to tell me she'd let you go down to South Carolina for a long weekend? How are you going to get around that one?" I sat back, confidant that I'd at least put a dent in her plans, but Dahlia didn't seem worried.

"No problem, baby." She grinned. "I'll tell her I'm spending the weekend with you. I mean, you're right, if she knew the truth she'd freak out, but she doesn't have to know, does she?"

Great. That wasn't going to work. I thought her plan was a terrible idea. And I didn't feel that comfortable with her lying to her mother either. What if something happened? But if her mind was made up, nothing I was going to say would stop her. I'd learned by now that she could be pretty stubborn. "I guess you want to borrow some money for the bus, and a hotel, right?"

Dahlia brightened. "I knew you'd come through for me. Listen, this is going to be as expensive as hell. The bus is one hundred and sixty dollars round-trip, and it's seventy-five dollars a night to stay at the tacky Holiday Inn that's near the base, but hey, it's only for one night. You know I'll pay you back, don't you? I don't even have to borrow all of that, I already have sixty dollars of my own."

"Dahlia, it's not the money. I just think it's dangerous, that's all. I mean, besides the fact that after all the hassle of getting down there he might not even see you! And don't you think there's a reason why your mother would freak out if she knew you were going down there? Jesus, don't you ever read the papers? It's just not that safe for a seventeen-year-old to go traveling around by herself!"

Dahlia blinked at me in surprise. "I know that, Stephanie, why do you think you're coming with me?"

CHAPTER TWELVE

Friday morning I woke up around five A.M. I tossed and turned for a while trying to get back to sleep, but I couldn't, so I decided I might as well get up and pack. To tell the truth, I was sort of excited about going away with Dahlia. It was an adventure of sorts: I felt like we were in a road movie or something.

I wandered into my dressing room to get stuff together for the trip. It was too bad we weren't going in disguise, or I could have used some of my old clothes. I brushed my hand through the rows and rows of sweaters that were folded over hangers so they wouldn't lose their shape. Fair Isle, mono-grammed, Shetland . . . they were what the idealized teenager selling toothpaste wore, so I had worn them too. I'd feel like a fool wearing a monogrammed sweater with penny loafers around Dahlia. I remem-bered what I'd told Dr. Steinhart about smell, and how powerful a sense memory it was. I leaned into the sweaters and took a deep breath. Maybe some scent lingered, something that would remind me of what my life used to be like when I was still acting, but the only thing I could get from them was the faint odor of mothballs. I felt slightly ridiculous smelling my clothes, trying to force some feeling. I decided I'd better focus on the matter at hand and started to pack.

I wasn't taking more than I could fit in my backpack. I didn't want my parents asking questions, which they definitely would if I left for school lugging a suitcase. I took my backpack with me every day, though, so I knew that wouldn't arouse any suspicions. Of course, the fact that I wasn't going to be home the entire weekend might give them a clue that I was up to something, but that had been surprisingly easy to work out. Dahlia had convinced me that the simplest solution was for me to tell my parents that I was going to spend the weekend with her, meanwhile she told her mother that she was going to be over at my house the whole time. I didn't think that was such a great idea. There was too much room for error. I mean, my parents could easily call up to check on me, or Dahlia's mother might decide to do the same with her. It was my parents who unknowingly smoothed the whole thing over by announcing that they were going away for the weekend themselves. Now all Dahlia and I had to do was beep in to my machine from the road. If either Dahlia's mother or my parents left a message, we'd call from a pay phone and say the music had been too loud for us to hear the phone. The only problem was that my parents weren't leaving until Saturday morning, which left Friday night wide open. I had told them that I was spending it at Dahlia's. Of course that could backfire, but I didn't think that even my parents would be so overprotective that they'd call and check on a one-night sleep-over. They'd been so happy when I told them I'd be sleeping over at Dahlia's house! It made me feel kind of guilty. What if they knew what I was really up to?

I emptied my backpack completely, so there'd be as much room as possible for my clothes. I put in my nightgown, some underwear and socks, and two extra shirts. What else did I need? I figured I'd be sitting in a hotel room most of the time—it wasn't as if I'd be going to any costume balls or anything. I looked around to see if I'd forgotten anything. The bus didn't leave until eight, but I wouldn't be home again. I tossed in my toothbrush and closed the pack. It looked pretty overstuffed. I hoped my parents wouldn't call me on it, although if they did, I'd just say I needed it all for my sleep-over. I threw on my jeans and wandered into the kitchen. My parents were already there drinking coffee.

"Good morning, Steph. Do you want some break-fast?" My mother looked up from the paper.

I usually don't have breakfast. But I'd be pretty busy all day with the details of the trip and wouldn't get a chance to eat before dinnertime. With that in mind I grabbed a bowl of cereal and sat down. It was a brand of a cereal that I'd auditioned for many times. That was one of the commercials that I'd never gotten a booking for, though. In the old days my mother had been hypersensitive about things like that. We didn't use Heinz ketchup for the four years in a row that they kept rejecting me.

"Are you sure you'll be all right on your own this weekend?"

"Sure, Mom," I mumbled into my cereal. I didn't want to dwell on the weekend with my parents.

"You can always ask Dahlia back here with you," she continued.

I nearly choked, if only she knew!

"You know, Steph." My father cleared his throat. "We wouldn't be going away this weekend unless we thought you could handle it. It seems like things are going a little smoother for you. We're very happy that you have this new friend."

Even though he was doing his would-be sitcom dad routine, it kind of got to me that they cared so much. All of a sudden I felt terrible. Here they thought I was doing so well, sleeping over at a friend's house like a normal kid, but the truth was completely different. I stood up abruptly. "I have to get going. I'll see you Monday, okay?" I was afraid that if I spent any more time with them I'd lose it. I grabbed my coat and backpack, and left for school.

Dahlia and I had decided on our game plan the night before. I had an appointment with Dr. Steinhart today, but I was going to leave school even earlier than usual so that I could go to the bank. I felt a little strange about cutting English—I'd only cut study hall before, but I figured that was the least of my sins. After the bank I had a few trip-related errands to run. I wanted to get some paperbacks to read on the bus, and stuff like that, and then I'd go to Dr. Steinhart's. I would meet up with Dahlia around five and we'd have dinner and then go to the bus station.

The day passed by pretty quickly. I alternated between feelings of excitement and disbelief. I really couldn't believe that I had let myself get talked into something this crazy. I finished biology, gave Dahlia the thumbs up when I passed her in the hall, and ducked out of school by two-thirty.

At the bank I asked for five hundred dollars in twenties. Two bus tickets at a hundred and sixty apiece, a hotel room at seventy-five, and a hundred in case of emergencies. We'd decided to use Dahlia's sixty bucks for food. I put four hundred and forty dollars in a money belt I'd just gotten. I didn't feel like waking up in South Carolina only to find that some jerk had gotten off the bus in the middle of the night, taking my backpack and money with him. The sixty I kept out was for the other errands.

I went to the Mystery Book Shop and got two of the latest best-selling thrillers. I love thrillers, but I hardly ever have the time to read them, not if I want to get any homework done. But I figured that two all-night bus trips, not to mention being alone while Dahlia was seeing Daryll, would be more than enough time to catch up.

I left the Mystery Book Shop and headed uptown toward Dr. Steinhart's and a fancy chocolate store. We would probably get hungry being on the road all night. At least it seemed like a good excuse for eating chocolate. I got a pound of assorted stuff. I was sure my skin would look great next week, but I didn't care.

I was starting to feel like a gangster in a forties movie getting supplies together before hitting the road on the run from the police. I couldn't think of any female buddy movies from back then, but if there had been, I was taking the Barbara Stanwyck part, while

Dahlia was doing Ida Lupino.

I spotted a stationery store two blocks from Dr. Steinhart's and went in to buy a deck of cards. I'd had to talk Dahlia out of lugging Pictionary with us, but maybe we could play gin or something. After all, it was a pretty long bus ride. Then I headed over to Dr. Steinhart's.

My mind had been so full of the trip that I hadn't thought that much about what had happened in our last session. I wished Dr. Steinhart had canceled today too, but he'd called the day before to confirm our appointment. All of a sudden I felt nervous. I was uncomfortable talking with him. I didn't want to think about what had come up last time. Maybe he wouldn't be in the mood either, but as he opened the door to his office, I could tell that he was plenty in the mood. I tried to stall by asking him how he was feeling, but he waved my questions aside.

"Have you had any more thoughts about what we talked about last session?"

"What's to think about?" I wasn't trying to be difficult, but what *was* there to think about? I'd told him what had happened to me, he couldn't fix the past, and that was that.

"There's quite a bit to think about, Stephanie. Besides everything else, there's your feelings regarding what happened. It's very important for you to identify how you see yourself based on what happened to you. Do you feel like a victim? That would be a natural although erroneous conclusion. Many people who've experienced the kind of trauma you have often feel ashamed and unworthy. It's not uncommon to perceive oneself as unclean."

Sometimes when Rob is talking, I just stare out the window and let what he says wash right over me, but now I snapped my head around and looked straight at him. "What did you just say?"

"That you can form conclusions that—"

"No, before that, you said that sometimes people feel different things."

"Yes, shame, guilt, feelings of self-hatred, of being dirty, used—"

"Well, aren't they?"

"Excuse me?"

"Aren't they?"

"Aren't they what?"

"Dirty, unclean!"

"Is that the way you feel?"

"No. I don't know. I don't want to talk about this anymore, it makes me sick!"

Rob looked concerned. "But you have to talk about this, Stephanie. What I said is true—it's not what happens to you, but how you interpret what happens to you, that is important. You're going to have to change your conclusions about the past if you're going to feel better and be able to get on with your life. If those are in fact the conclusions that you've drawn, then it's important that you've identified them. But that's not enough, you have to see that there are other interpretations."

"It's not that easy! I can't just change the way I feel! What do you mean, 'other interpretations'! What am I supposed to think?"

"I didn't say it would be easy to change your conclusions, Stephanie, I said it was necessary. As for coming up with other interpretations, it's important that you think of some."

"Well, I can't," I said. I was so used to feeling the way I did, I didn't see how I could feel any different at this point. Still, if I could, that would be wonderful. I'd love not to feel ashamed the next time a boy tried to dance with me. I'd love to be able to hold my head up and look anyone in the eye without feeling they could see all the scars that were inside me.

"That's a knee-jerk reaction. You need to give this some thought. If it's hard for you to be put on the spot like this, I understand, but I'd like to give you some homework, okay?"

I shrugged. I figured I could always do it in the hotel room.

"I want you, just as an intellectual exercise, to see if you can draw any other conclusions. Pretend that you've been told this story by someone else: How would you react to it? Would you think the same things about them? See what you come up with."

I nodded. I could see what he was getting at but I didn't agree, and anyway it was time for me to go.

"Stephanie," Dr. Steinhart said as I was opening the door. "Take it easy this weekend. Now is the time to be good to yourself, take some long walks, have a fancy meal, go to an exhibit you've been wanting to see. But be careful with yourself—after what you've dealt with this week you're like an open wound. Don't do anything that will stir all this up."

I paused with my hand on the doorknob. For a moment I was worried, but I shrugged my shoulders. What could possibly happen to me in South Carolina?

CHAPTER THIRTEEN

"Gin."

"I don't believe it! You must be cheating!"

Dahlia giggled wickedly. "Face it, I'm a genius."

"It's a good thing we're only playing for a penny a point, otherwise I'd be wiped out by now."

"I told you we should have brought Pictionary."

"Yeah, well, let's call it quits for now, okay? I want to read for a while."

"Spoilsport," Dahlia said good-naturedly. She dug into the bag of chocolates.

"Hey, save some of those for later, all right? We've got a really long trip ahead of us." That was for sure. We'd been on the road for about two hours and already my legs were getting cramped, but so far everything had gone like clockwork. I'd met Dahlia at five o'clock and we'd had some dinner before heading over to the Port Authority Bus Terminal. I'd been shocked at the suitcase Dahlia was carrying. She must have had enough stuff in there for a six-week trip. "What is that?" I'd shrieked when I saw her lugging it down the street.

"I need different outfits! Besides, I couldn't figure out what to wear when I meet Daryll. I figured I'd bring it all and you could help me decide."

"Didn't your mother wonder why you needed all that for a weekend?"

Dahlia shrugged. "I told her we wanted to trade some clothes."

"Just don't make me carry it, okay?"

Dahlia had laughed, but it hadn't been that easy to drag her suitcase all through the Port Authority. We'd needed the bus driver's help to shove it up on the luggage rack, where it was threatening to fall on our heads.

"Say, when is the first stop, anyway?" Dahlia interrupted my thoughts.

"What do you care? We're staying on this thing all night, remember? You're not going to start doing an 'are we there yet,' are you?"

"What do you think I am, five years old? I just want to get out and stretch my legs, maybe get a cup of coffee or something."

That actually sounded good. "Why don't you ask the driver, or figure it out from the schedule or something? I'm trying to read."

"You're only on the first page!" Dahlia grumbled, but she got up and walked unsteadily to the front of the bus.

"Twenty minutes," she announced triumphantly, sitting down again. "I wonder how—"

"Dahlia, I'm just starting to get into this; it's a really good thriller. Do you mind letting me read?" I said impatiently.

"C'mon, talk to me, I don't have anything to read, and I'm bored. I'll probably go to sleep after this stop, you can read then."

I put the book down with a theatrical sigh. "Okay, so talk."

"I'm starting to get nervous, you know? What if this doesn't work?"

"Oh, no! Dahlia, don't do this to me! I told you this was crazy! I can't believe you talked me into this, and now you're not even sure!" The only reason I'd let her talk me into this whole thing was because she'd seemed so convinced that she was doing the right thing.

"Relax! I didn't say I wasn't sure. I just said I was nervous, that's all."

"Well, if you're so sure that this is a great idea, why are you so nervous?"

"I'm not that nervous, I'm just getting kind of

excited about seeing him, that's all. What's with you? You act like you're picking on me."

She sounded irritated, as if she was spoiling for an argument. That was the last thing I wanted right now. To tell the truth, I hadn't really wanted to read, I wanted to think about what Dr. Steinhart had said before in my session, and I couldn't do that and talk to Dahlia at the same time. I would think about it after she went to sleep, but I didn't want to tire myself out first by arguing.

"Let's drop it, okay?"

"Sure, I'm sorry if I sounded nasty. You're really helping me out here, you know? And it's not just the money, either."

I yawned hugely. "God, I really need some coffee, not to mention the bathroom. I hope we get to whatever this little boondocky bus stop is soon."

"There's a bathroom on the bus."

"Yeah, it smells like the monkey house at the zoo. I bet you could get a disease from the door handle."

Dahlia laughed. "Well, I don't think you have to wait much longer. I think we're slowing down."

She was right. The bus driver made an announcement over the loudspeaker: "Ladies and gentlemen, we're pulling into Greensboro Point. We will be making a twenty-minute stop. For those of you who are making Greensboro your final stop, thank you for traveling with Greyhound."

Dahlia and I hopped off the bus.

"I'm going to call my parents now, okay?"

"What are you, crazy?"

"No, I just want to check and make sure that your mother hasn't called my house or vice versa."

"You better make sure you have enough change; it won't sound too believable to say that you're at my house, if the long distance operator cuts in."

I laughed. She was right. I got ten dollars' worth of quarters while Dahlia got us coffee, and we arranged to meet back on the bus.

I shoved the quarters into the pay phone and waited anxiously while it rang. What if something had gone wrong? My mother picked up on the third ring.

"Hi, Mom. I just thought I'd call and say good night."

"Stephanie? Are you all right?" She sounded worried.

Shit, had we screwed up?

"Of course I'm all right. How come?" I asked warily.

"Well, honey, I'm just surprised you called, that's all." She sounded touched.

Great. Now I felt like a total jerk. Well, at least the plan was going through without any problems.

"Stephanie, are you still there? What's all that noise I hear?"

I was in an enclosed phone booth, but there were a lot of people milling around, not to mention the fact that they had just announced that the bus was leaving in five minutes.

"Umm, it's nothing, just the TV. Look, I've got to go. I'll see you Monday. Good night."

"Good night, Steph."

I hung up the phone. I just had time to dash to the bathroom before getting back on the bus.

"It looks like everything's working out," I said as I slid back into my seat next to Dahlia.

"My mother didn't call your house or anything?"

"Nope."

"Fantastic! That's the only thing that could have gone wrong. Phew, we're in the clear now, girl."

I didn't quite share Dahlia's enthusiasm, but it was hard not to agree. After all, tonight was the most likely time for things to have gotten screwed up. There was no way that Dahlia's mother would call mine after ten o'clock. I guess we really were in the clear.

"I can relax now. I'm going to try and sleep. Go back to your thriller."

Dahlia closed her eyes, leaving me to my book. I put it down and tried to remember some of the things that Dr. Steinhart had said. I thought about the home-work he'd given me. What other conclusions would I come up with if I heard the same story about someone else? I didn't think that I was being unduly hard on myself. After all, I'd been there; Dr. Steinhart hadn't. I wanted to believe him, though, and that surprised me. Maybe I was getting tired of feeling the way I did. Maybe I was getting tired of having everybody treat me as if I were some fragile piece of glass. In some ways I was jealous of Dahlia. It must be nice to care about somebody so much that you'd do anything to get him back. I wished that I felt okay enough to have a boyfriend. I thought about Tim. I hardly knew him, but I kept thinking back to the way his arm had felt on mine, right before I saw my scar. I wondered what it would be like to kiss him. I knew I wouldn't feel com-fortable doing anything like that right now, but sup-pose, just suppose, Dr. Steinhart was right, what then? Would I "get well" again? Would I be able to have a boyfriend then? Could I go back to acting?

It was getting pretty late. It was pitch-dark outside the bus, and most of the passengers were asleep. The wheels had a soothing rhythm, and I started to close my eyes.

I had finally dozed off for a few minutes, when I was woken up by a sharp bump.

"Folks, it looks like we might have a little problem here. We'll be able to make it to the next scheduled stop, and I'll see what's going on when we get there," the bus driver announced to a chorus of groans.

"What's going on?" Dahlia mumbled sleepily.

"I don't know, there's a problem with the bus or something. The driver's going to take a look at the next stop."

"I hope he makes it that far." Dahlia looked worried.

"Don't worry, he said he would, and anyway it's only about ten minutes away from here." But I didn't feel that great about it either. We'd better make it to the next stop. I didn't want to walk anywhere with Dahlia's monster suitcase.

The bus pulled up outside the station complex, which included a Howard Johnson's restaurant and motel. At least we wouldn't have to sleep in the station if anything was really wrong with the bus.

"Okay, folks, listen up," the bus driver said. "We may be here a bit while I figure out what the problem is. For those of you who were planning to continue, I ask that you be a little patient. Get something to eat, relax, and I'll keep you posted."

Everyone grumbled, but there wasn't much we could do about the situation. We all trooped out into the coffee shop adjoining the station.

"Do you want to split a hot fudge sundae? I haven't been in a Hojo's for years." I think the last time was when I was on location for some regional commercial up in Buffalo. "Dahlia?" She didn't look too thrilled with my idea. "What's wrong?"

"What do you mean what's wrong? This whole weekend is falling apart! We planned everything, and now the bus has to break down! What are we going to do?" she wailed.

"Come on, Dahlia, it's not that bad. Probably the bus driver can fix it. So we get in at ten A.M. instead of at eight. What's the big deal? At least we can stretch our legs for a while and eat something. You slept most of the time, but I was getting pretty uncomfortable."

"How can you say it's not a big deal? What if the bus doesn't get in until eleven-thirty or something? It's going to take me an hour to get ready, and visiting hours are only from ten until one!"

"Okay, okay, calm down. Why don't we wait and see what's going on with the bus before you get all carried away."

Dahlia shrugged her shoulders. She realized that I was right, and we couldn't do anything but wait and see. She cheered up when the waitress brought our sundae over.

"I'm gonna get a thousand cavities this weekend, first the chocolate on the bus, now this. And there's nothing to eat but McDonald's near the base."

"McDonald's won't give you cavities," I said, spooning up some hot fudge sauce.

"Yeah, but it will sure finish off my skin."

I was about to answer her when I noticed that the bus driver was entering the station.

"Hey, the driver's just come back. Let's finish this later. Come on." We both ran into the station. I wasn't worried about the waitress thinking we were running off without paying; it was pretty obvious what was going on.

Everyone gathered around the driver. "I'm very sorry. I know this is a big inconvenience, but there's a problem with the brakes, and I don't think it's safe to keep going. You can all put up here overnight. Greyhound will refund you completely, and we should be able to get a new bus over here in the morning."

Of course everybody started moaning and complaining, but there was nothing we could do. I wasn't that upset; it would be a lot nicer to sleep in a clean Howard Johnson's than stay on the bus all night.

"Come on, let's go back to the coffee shop and pay. We can check in after everyone else." There was already a line at the reception desk. It was one A.M., and there was only one tired clerk on duty.

We dragged our stuff into the restaurant, falling over each other and the suitcase. I signaled to the waitress.

"Anything else, ladies? I heard about the trouble. Too bad."

I was about to say no, that we didn't want anything else, when Dahlia piped up.

"Yeah, two cups of coffee would be great." The waitress nodded and left.

"Dahlia, are you crazy? I'm exhausted, the last thing I want is coffee; let's just go to bed." I figured that she'd be pretty upset about what was happening, but that she'd just get over it, and check in for the night. But there was a gleam in her eyes that was making me nervous. I hoped that she wasn't going to come up with any crazy ideas, because I barely had enough energy to keep my eyes open, let alone talk her out of some ridiculous new scheme.

"Go to bed? No way! We've got to work something out. We can't stay here tonight! I've got to be in South Carolina tomorrow morning!"

"Dahlia, I know you're really upset, but what can we do? Can't you just see him Sunday?"

"I didn't come all this way to screw up now! And no, I can't just see him Sunday! Okay? They only have open visiting for an hour on Sunday; that's not enough time!"

"Okay, Dahlia, you don't want to stay here tonight, fine. What do you suggest we do instead?" I said. I hoped that she wouldn't be able to give me an answer.

"Look, don't start screaming or anything, but maybe we could hitchhike or something."

"Hitchhike? Are you insane? For godsakes, I wouldn't hitchhike in broad daylight, let alone at one in the morning! Talk about not safe! Look, let's just get a room and go to sleep. We'll think of something in the morning." This was much, much worse than I had thought. It had never occurred to me that Dahlia would want to do anything *that* crazy. I thought that maybe she would want us to try and hire a car or something. That would have been outrageous enough, but the last thing I was going to do was hitchhike. I shivered just thinking about it. I was starting to feel pretty creepy just sitting in the coffee shop. Everyone else from the bus had already gone up to their rooms. The station was empty and so was the coffee shop, except for a couple of truck drivers having a late-night meal.

"Maybe you're right, I don't know. I just feel so miserable." Dahlia started to cry. I wasn't glad that she was crying, but I was glad that she seemed to be weakening.

"Now, there's a sight I hate to see."

I looked up. Some redneck truck driver. Great. He had biceps that would rival Arnold Schwarzenegger's, and he looked like he should be wearing a sign that said TROUBLE.

"A pretty lady crying just breaks my heart."

"Listen, mister, we're really busy right now—"

"The name's Rick, honey. I couldn't help but overhear what you were saying. You know, I just bet I could help you little ladies."

I really wished he'd leave us alone. "Yeah, well, we're not little ladies, and—"

"Wait a minute, Stephanie." Dahlia looked at me beseechingly. "Let's hear what he has to say."

I tried to give Dahlia a vicious kick under the table, but succeeded only in bashing my shin.

"Well, I've got to be in South Carolina myself in the morning. I'm driving right through the night and I could use some company."

I shook my head at Dahlia. No, *no way*. Dahlia ignored me and flashed redneck Rick her most charming smile.

"Well, I have to get down there too, Mr. . . . ."

"Rick, sweetheart. I told you, the name's Rick."

"Look," I cut in, "we really don't want to hitchhike, okay? So thanks for the offer, but no thanks."

"Hey, I understand where you're coming from. It's not safe to hang around a deserted highway in the middle of the night. That's why you should come with me."

"He has a point, Stephanie."

"Dahlia," I said through gritted teeth, "can we talk by ourselves for a few minutes?"

"Sure, you two decide what you want. Hey, I'm just trying to do you gals a favor. I'll be inside the station if you need me." He ambled off.

"Look, Stephanie, you're right, hitching was a stupid idea, but this is perfect!"

"What do you think *this* is? A tea party? Where I come from, *this* is called hitchhiking!" I wanted to strangle Dahlia. I wondered if I was strong enough to drag her upstairs into a room.

"Sometimes you're so straight, you know that? Look, this is completely different. I mean, he's right, hitching is hanging out on the road waiting for whatever skeevy guy will pick you up. But we know this guy, it's totally different."

"What do you mean we know him? We just met him!"

"I just mean that it's okay. Look, this guy's a truck driver, right?"

"So?"

"So he's not going to do anything; he'd lose his job!"

I supposed that was true, but it didn't make me feel any better. It wasn't exactly as if it was a guarantee that he wouldn't try anything. The whole thing was too risky.

"Listen to me for a sec—" I started to say, but Dahlia cut me off.

"I'm going to go tell him that we're coming with him. You worry too much, I'm always telling you that. It'll be fine." She got up and went into the station. I could see her walk up to meet him. He put a hand on her arm and they sat down out of my view. I decided I'd give her a few minutes. We'd both been on edge. Then I'd walk in and, whether I was strong enough or not, drag her back to the lobby, where we'd get a room. I took a sip of my coffee; it was stone-cold by now. At this point I really did need some caffeine. The waitress was nowhere to be seen. I was the only one around. I walked behind the counter and poured myself another cup. It was scalding. I blew on it for a few seconds. I figured Dahlia had been alone with that creep long enough and walked toward the station.

The bus station was as deserted as the coffee shop had been. By now it was well after two in the morning. But where was Dahlia? She wouldn't leave me, would she? Just when I was starting to get scared, I heard a little noise. It was only a ghost of a cry, but it sent chills up my spine. I knew that noise, I knew it from my memories. I looked around frantically. There was a dark little hallway to the left. I ran toward it. Dahlia was there. So was the truck driver. He had her shoved against the wall. His hands were all over her. One of them was covering her mouth. The other was tearing off her shirt.

CHAPTER FOURTEEN

When I look back on it now, I realize that I probably stood there only for about a second before I reacted. But while it was going on, it seemed endless, like time stood still. I don't know how to explain what happened to me. Maybe it was that I had finally started telling Dr. Steinhart what had really happened, and my mind was naturally suggestible. Maybe it was like he had said, and I was an open wound. Or maybe it was the steam from the coffee I was carrying that helped to obscure everything.

All I know is that everything was a blur. I could hear Rick's voice yelling at Dahlia, and I could hear her, too. But there was someone else, who was it? And then, louder than all the rest, I heard it. I couldn't make out what the other voices were saying, but that last voice . . . "Nooo, please stop! Let go, you're hurting me!" Was that Dahlia? But it couldn't be. Both she and Rick had turned to look at me, and they were both staring silently. Rick looked frightened, like he had seen a ghost. I didn't know why he looked scared. He wasn't being hurt. But I was. . . . My arm! It was being twisted. . . . I could feel it being burned. And that voice! It wouldn't stop. It kept crying. "Please . . . stop that . . . you're hurting me! Please . . ."

"What's wrong with your friend? Is she some kind of retard?" That was Rick talking. His voice jarred me. All of a sudden I knew that other voice. I'd heard it before in Jim's class. It was the five-year-old me. But she wasn't talking anymore. The burning that I'd been feeling wasn't there anymore either. Instead what I felt was the steam from the boiling-hot coffee I was carrying.

"Duck!" I shrieked at Dahlia.

I don't know if Dahlia realized what I meant, but the sound of my real voice surprised her. And she jerked her head back. That was all I needed. With Dahlia's face averted, I threw the cup of boiling-hot coffee right at Rick.

"Jesus Christ!" he yelled. Temporarily blinded, he let go of Dahlia. I grabbed her and we ran into the hotel lobby. I rang the bell frantically.

"Help! Help!" I shouted.

After what seemed like hours, a sleepy desk clerk came out. "What the hell's going on?" he asked irritably.

I explained to him quickly. Dahlia wasn't saying anything—she seemed to be in shock. The clerk got a nasty-looking shovel out from behind the desk and went into the station. He came back a few seconds later, shaking his head. "The guy must have driven away."

"How could he drive? I practically blinded him!"

"Yeah, well, that's not going to stop a truck driver. I've seen some of 'em drive when they were practically asleep." He chuckled. "Seriously, though, you must have scared the hell out of him. He probably figures you're going to call the cops. You should, too."

I looked at Dahlia. She shook her head slightly.

"We don't even know his last name, or his license plate, or what company he drove for."

"Well, let's just hope you frightened him from doing anything like that again."

Dahlia and I checked in and went up to our room. She seemed pretty subdued, and I wondered if she was in shock. She wandered around looking in closets and turning on faucets. I asked her if she wanted a doctor.

"What for?"

"Well, you seem pretty upset. I mean, believe me, I can understand why and everything."

"I don't need a doctor; nothing happened to me.

I'm just scared thinking about what could have happened. It's funny, I've lived in New York my whole life, and nothing like this has ever happened. I can't believe it. It's my fault, too. I shouldn't have trusted the guy. You were right. If you hadn't come along I don't know what I would have done." Dahlia paused. "I . . . well, you really saved me, Stephanie, and I don't know how to thank you. But what was going on with you? I mean, before you told me to duck. What was that?"

I was lying on the bed staring up at the ceiling. I felt drained. I was listening to her, but thinking about myself, too. Now I turned to look at her. It wasn't her question that had caught my attention, though I realized that I'd have some explaining to do. It was what she said about it being her fault.

I thought about what Dr. Steinhart had said earlier. He said that my conclusions about what happened to me were erroneous. That people often felt the way I did, or if they didn't, then they made other judgments that were just as false. I'd wanted to believe him, but I hadn't been able to. Now listening to Dahlia, his words made sense. How ridiculous that she would think that what had happened was her fault! I thought back to the scene in the bus station. I'd been scared. I'd been angry at Dahlia for getting us into such a dangerous situation. But never once did it occur to me that she was guilty. It never crossed my mind that she had "asked for it." I knew what Steinhart had been getting at when he asked me to do the homework. It made no more sense for Dahlia to come to the conclusion that it was her fault than it did for her to think that the moon was made of green cheese. It made no more sense for Dahlia to think it was her fault than it did for me to think I was filthy and scarred. Unbelievable but true. It was as if Dahlia were holding up a mirror. I'd looked in that mirror for a long time; it had been filled with shadows and smoke, but now it was crystal clear. I felt light-headed. I felt better than I had in an entire year. More than anything I wished that it hadn't taken Dahlia having such a horrible experience to make me see the light. But at least I could try and make sure that she didn't have the same problems I did.

"It's not your fault!" I said vehemently, sitting up on the bed.

Dahlia looked surprised at how forceful I sounded. "Yes, it was, Stephanie. I shouldn't have gone off with him, I—"

"No! You're wrong!" I jumped up and grabbed Dahlia by the shoulders. "Well, okay, you should have more sense than to go off with a truck driver, but the rest of it . . . you're wrong, it wasn't your fault! Why don't you think Rick is to blame instead? Isn't he the one who did something wrong? Shouldn't you be blaming *him*?"

Dahlia gave me a half smile. "What makes you so smart all of a sudden? Stephanie . . ." Her smile faded.

"Yeah?"

"What happened with you out there? I mean, you sort of went crazy. What was that? Are you sure that *you're* okay?"

"I'm okay." I smiled. I really felt like maybe for once that was the truth, too. Dahlia looked unconvinced, though. I took a deep breath. "Listen, Dahlia, you know that I've had a bunch of problems; what happened out there, well, it set some things off for me. I had something sort of like what happened to you happen to me a long time ago. But I don't want to talk about that right now; believe me, I'm working it out in therapy. The important thing is that you're okay."

Dahlia looked uncomfortable, like she wanted to say something but didn't know how to. She shrugged her shoulders. "I see what you mean about how if anything had happened, it wouldn't be my fault. But still, I did act pretty stupid, and you did save me. If you hadn't been there with that coffee, or whatever it was that you threw at him, I don't know how I would have been able to get away."

"It was just luck, that's all. It was lucky that I was

holding something that scalding, and it was lucky that my reflexes kicked in."

Dahlia shook her head. "I don't think so. I don't think I would have thought of it. I think you're stronger than you know."

Maybe she was right.

"Anyway," Dahlia continued, "I'd like to put this whole thing out of my head right now. Steph?"

"Yeah?"

"Well, look, about this trip, we don't have to go on tomorrow."

"Are you serious? After all this? I thought you had to see Daryll. Don't you at least want the one hour on Sunday?"

"Yeah, well, in a way I'd still like to visit him, but tonight made some things clear to me, too. I mean, it's not Daryll's fault that I was in that situation or anything, but, well, maybe I don't want to go out with a guy who'll break up with me without even giving me a chance to explain. Maybe we should just go back to the city, you know? I don't feel that safe going on right now."

"Well, you won't get much of an argument from me about that."

"We could stay at your apartment for real now, right? I mean that would be okay, wouldn't it?"

"Sure, we could go to the museum or something," I said, thinking of Dr. Steinhart's advice.

"*The museum?* Well, I guess I owe you."

I closed my eyes. I was glad we weren't going to talk about anything else for a while. I was pretty talked out, and besides, I wanted to let all the things that I'd just realized marinate for a while. Dahlia got up restlessly and started flipping through the movie guide that was on top of the television.

"Hey, that guy we like is on."

"Who?"

"You know the one, Laurence Olivier."

"You're kidding. In what?"

"Something called *That Hamilton Woman.*"

"Are you joking? That's the best!"

"Well, it starts in ten minutes." She paused. "Stephanie, I'll never really be able to thank you. Besides saving my ass and everything. What you said about it not being my fault . . . that was the best thing you could have told me."

"You know what, Dahlia, I'll never be able to thank you either. You did something for me tonight too." She really had. I wondered if I would have come to understand my feelings on my own, if tonight had never happened.

"Hey, I don't see that I did anything so special, but

if I did, then it's the least I could do." She paused. "So do you want to watch the movie, or what?"

"Of course!"

"There's a vending machine down the hall. Why don't we get some stuff for the movie."

So we went down the hall and got a bunch of chips from the vending machine and munched our way through *That Hamilton Woman.* There were a couple of great old movies in a row, and we were both too wired to sleep, so we made a marathon of it.

And the next morning we got on a bus to New York and slept the whole way back.

CHAPTER FIFTEEN

All day Monday, I kept wondering what I should tell Dr. Steinhart. In a way, I had done the homework that he'd asked me to. Seeing what happened to Dahlia and the way she started blaming herself made the whole thing seem so much clearer. Maybe Rob was right, maybe what happened to me hadn't been my fault. I wasn't completely sure that was true, but at least now I was willing to see the possibility. Anyway, I wasn't sure how I was going to tell him about my weekend trip, but for once I really felt like I wanted to talk.

I got to my appointment twenty minutes early, and sat in the waiting room thinking of how I was going to start. I shouldn't have worried, though, because Dr. Steinhart began asking me questions right away.

"Did you think about what we discussed last week?"

I nodded.

"Well, what thoughts came up? Were you able to come to any different conclusions?"

"I think so. You might be right, about people in my situation coming to erroneous conclusions."

Rob looked pretty surprised at that. In fact he gave me a look I'd never seen before. I couldn't help laughing.

"Why do you seem so shocked? I thought you'd be pleased."

"I am," he recovered. "But I'm also surprised. In most cases it takes a while to change certain damaging beliefs. I'm curious. What made you feel differently?"

"Well, it's sort of a long story."

"We've hardly even begun the session."

"You promise that you won't tell my parents?"

"You know that therapy is confidential, Stephanie."

"Well, I haven't really talked much about my friend Dahlia, but you've heard me mention her, right?"

"Yes."

"I went away with her this weekend, to visit her boyfriend down in South Carolina. My parents don't know or anything. Anyway, on the way there the bus broke down, and some gross truck driver offered to give us a ride. I said no, but Dahlia really wanted to go with him. She went off to talk with him about it, and he, well, he tried to attack her. She's okay, though, I mean nothing really happened," I said quickly when I noticed how shocked Rob was looking. "It's just that after, when I saw how she was reacting, I could see what you'd been talking about. I mean, she hadn't done anything wrong, and yet she was blaming herself. I'm still not sure, it's just that I figure if Dahlia was wrong about herself, maybe I was wrong about myself, too." I paused and sat back. Old Rob looked kind of stunned. I guess that wasn't too surprising; I'd probably just said more than I had the entire time I'd been in therapy. Not only that, but it sounded pretty dramatic, too.

"You went down to South Carolina?" Rob shook his head as if he were trying to clear out the cobwebs. It seemed like a strange response, but I guess he was just trying to get a handle on the tangible details.

"Well, no, we didn't get all the way there. I told you the bus broke down, that's how all this happened."

"You say Dahlia is all right—how did she get away from the truck driver? What happened?"

"I surprised him with a cup of hot coffee, right in his face. Then Dahlia and I ran away." I shivered. I didn't like remembering it.

"You were there?"

I nodded.

"And you saved her? That was extremely brave of you. Especially considering your own experiences, it must have been quite traumatic."

I shrugged. Extremely brave? I certainly didn't think of it in those terms. As for being traumatic, I'll say. I know that part of the reason I was able to blind Rick was because I'd confused him when I started floating in and out. "It was sort of traumatic," I told Dr. Steinhart. "I sort of had a flashback for a second, but I snapped out of it pretty quickly."

"What kind of flashback?"

"Almost like I had in sense memory that time. I went back to being five years old again."

"But this time you were able to get out of it."

It was a statement, not a question, and I realized he was right. I had snapped out of it when I heard Rick. I'd been able to function, it hadn't really been like the time in acting class at all. That had been the beginning of my problems, this time it seemed like it was almost a signal of the end. "I guess you're right, I hadn't thought about that, but it's not like everything's fine or anything. There's still a lot of work I have to do." I was surprised that I said that.

Dr. Steinhart laughed. "I don't tend to think of people as getting completely 'cured,' but I do think that you've made significant progress, Stephanie. I think now we can really get down to work. I'm honestly quite shocked that you would do something as reckless as this trip, but it does sound as if the end result was beneficial. I'd say you had what some therapists refer to as a conversion experience."

"A conversion experience?"

"That's what it's called."

"Does it have anything to do with religion?"

"In a way; it's where the expression comes from. People don't convert from one faith to another because they've weighed all the pros and cons of each particular creed. Rather, they have a blinding flash of insight, something that changes the way they look at things. Something like what you've had. Of course, you have been laying the groundwork in therapy, but it does seem as if this experience has led you to some new conclusions."

"But I still have some of the same feelings I did before," I protested. "Things just feel different somehow."

"I'm sure you do, Stephanie. Getting over the kind of experience you've had is never easy, but you've had a real breakthrough. But I must add that although I would never break the bounds of therapy and tell your parents what you did over the weekend, I find it very disturbing. Please don't ever do anything like that again without telling someone. If you don't feel you can tell your parents, at least discuss it with me."

"You don't have to worry, I'll never do anything like that again." That was for sure.

"In any case, let's pick up with this on Wednesday," Dr. Steinhart said, holding the door open. The session was over. I started to walk home lost in thought. I hadn't seen my parents since Friday morning. They'd be returning home from their trip now, and I couldn't decide what, if anything, to tell them. On the one hand, I knew I couldn't tell them the truth, not if I didn't want to be grounded for the next twenty-five years.

On the other hand, I wanted to let them know something. If not what really happened, at least that I was feeling a little better. The more I thought about it, the more I realized that the past year had been pretty hard for them, too. It couldn't have been that fun knowing that their daughter was unhappy all the time, and not really knowing how to help her. Still, I didn't exactly know what to do. I wasn't going to tell them about any "conversion experience" or anything. Besides the fact that I wasn't going to let them in on Dahlia's and my little adventure. I'd never been the kind to tell my parents *everything*, anyway. That wasn't the way that we'd been close.

I arrived home just as my parents were getting back. My mother was in the foyer looking over the mail, and my father was carrying their suitcase back to their room.

"Hi, honey," my mother said, looking up from the bills. "Did you have a good time with Dahlia this weekend?"

"Uh, yeah" was all that I could think of saying. I guessed my true confessions didn't all have to come tumbling out right away. Maybe I'd think of how and what to tell them before dinner. My father came into the hall and I could see him arranging his face into its sitcom mode. I felt irritated. But for once I was just as annoyed with myself as I was with my parents. I felt like I needed to do something right away to get things back on track. I'd done a lot of thinking, and I could sort of understand my parents better now. After all, if I hadn't been able to stop Dahlia's attacker, I knew just how I would have felt. Besides being angry, and sad for her, the overwhelming feeling I would have had would have been a selfish one. I would have felt uncomfortable. I would have felt uneasy being around her. It's sad but true. I would have felt like she'd been through something that I'd been powerless to prevent, and it would have created a gulf between us. I could see now how my parents must have felt. Their world had been destroyed too that afternoon that Jim had brought me home. For so long, all I'd thought about was how horrible it was that this thing had happened to *me*. I never thought how my parents must have felt when they realized that the perfect childhood they thought they'd provided for me never existed. Anyway, I wanted to get everything back on a more even keel. Maybe things wouldn't be the same, but they could be a little bit better, couldn't they?

"Did you do anything special this weekend with Dahlia?" Mom asked.

"Uh, no, not really." If they only knew!

"So what did you do?" my father chimed in. "Did you see any good movies?"

"We saw a couple old ones on TV." I was starting to feel like I was in an old movie myself. Maybe *Waterloo Bridge*, with Vivien Leigh, or a really sappy Deborah Kerr one. The kind where the heroine has some secret, and if she only told the right people everything would be all right, but she doesn't tell the right people, and because she doesn't, some completely avoidable tragedy occurs. I've always hated those movies. But nothing tragic was going to happen now. I just wished that I could think of something to say that would break down this wall that had been between me and my parents for the past year.

"Hey, Mom, do you want to go to a matinee on Wednesday? I could cancel Dr. Steinhart for once."

My mother looked surprised. Well, I guess that did sort of come out of nowhere. Maybe I should have led up to it or something.

"Well, sure, honey, you know I'd love to go to a show with you. Is there something you want to see especially?"

I had no idea what was on Broadway right now, but that wasn't the point. I just wanted to have an afternoon like we used to, but I felt too uncomfortable saying things like that. Whatever else we had been as a family, we certainly hadn't been given to saying mushy things, or being all lovey-dovey. I was wondering what I should say next when the phone rang.

My mother picked it up. She got a funny look on her face for a second, and then handed it to me. "It's for you," she said, giving me a weird look. It couldn't be Dahlia, or my mother would have recognized her voice.

"Hello?"

"Stephanie?" I didn't recognize the voice, but it was a guy, at least it sounded like it was, it was hard to tell, because whoever it was, they were having a hard time clearing their throat.

"Yeah?"

"Um, hi, this is Tim . . . remember, I'm in your French class? I got your number from Dahlia. We have geometry together, and I always see you hanging out together, so I figured she'd know it. Anyway, listen, you seemed pretty distracted at the dance the other night, but I figured any girl who could guess that I was Heathcliff had to be all right. Do you want to get together? I'm figuring if you knew *Wuthering Heights*, you're probably into old movies. Would you like to go and see one sometime? Maybe this Friday?"

I looked at my parents; they were staring at me openmouthed. They were totally focused on me. I could see that my mother had scrawled "a boy" on a piece of memo paper and shoved it in front of my father. Well, I guess they would be pretty surprised, considering the number of phone calls I'd been getting from guys in the past couple years. I felt a flash of irritation. Would they ever treat me as if I were normal? Suddenly I knew how I was going to let them know that things were better. The thing that would make Tim happiest, that would make me happiest, would also make them happiest. All I had to do was the very thing I'd been thinking about on and off for the past week.

"Stephanie, are you there?" Tim sounded nervous.

"Sure, Tim, I'm right here. I'd love to go. Do you know what's playing?"

"Well, if you're into old movies, there's a Clark

Gable festival over at the Film Forum. How about *It Happened One Night?*"

"I love that one! That would be great!" We made arrangements about where to meet after classes on Friday and I hung up the phone.

I was so high from my conversation with Tim, I didn't even notice that my parents were staring at me.

I was really excited about going out with Tim. It would be my first date! But even beyond the fact that I was looking forward to going out with someone who was imaginative enough to dress up as Heathcliff, my accepting a date with a guy was a major breakthrough. It was a milepost on the road to recovery. I knew that there was nothing I could do or say to my parents that could make the general state of things any clearer.

And from the look on my parents' faces, they knew it too.

CHAPTER SIXTEEN

"Stephanie? You're Stephanie Holt, aren't you?"

"Yes."

But who was she? She was a teacher or something, but I didn't have her for any of my classes.

"We haven't had a chance to talk. I'm Mrs. Jenkins, the guidance counselor."

"Oh, okay." What did she want?

"You're graduating next January, aren't you?"

"Yes."

"Well, most seniors come and talk to me in September about colleges, but next September will be a little late for you. It's best to think about these things about a year in advance. Do you think maybe we could have a chat after the Christmas break?"

"Sure." College. I guess that's what normal people did.

"I've heard that you're an actress. You might like to think about Yale."

Yale. I didn't think my grades would be up to it, but

still it was something to consider. Maybe I would apply and maybe I wouldn't, but I knew one thing for sure, I was going to go back to acting. Maybe not right away, maybe not for a few years, but someday I'd want to again. Oh, not to commercials, and not to some snooty acting school where they encouraged you to spill your guts all over the place either. No, sir, not for me, not anymore. When I went back to acting, I'd find my own niche. That was something else I'd figured out. For so long I'd felt like an outsider. I never fit in at my old school, I never fit in at my acting classes, and I didn't really feel like I fit in here either. But somehow, none of that stuff seemed to matter anymore. It was as if all of a sudden I knew who I was. I was somebody who'd been through a lot. I'd gotten thrown for a while, but I was back on course now. And I felt pretty solid.

But I don't want to pretend like everything was perfect, because if you ask me, my life still had a million problems. Now, though, more than ever they seem like the problems that other teenagers might have. Like the fact I'd gained three pounds from all the junk food Dahlia and I had eaten over that weekend. Or what about the surprise math quiz that I was sure I failed earlier? How likely would Yale be with grades like that? And besides everything else, I was really nervous about my date with Tim. Rob had been pretty impressed that I was going out with a guy. I'd been really happy about it too, but right now the butterflies in my stomach had the upper hand. It was Friday and we were going to meet by the front door. I figured that I looked all right, at least. Dahlia had come over the night before to help me pick out an outfit. It had taken hours trying to figure out what I should wear, but we'd finally come up with a couple possibilities. Then I'd woken up in the morning and spent another half an hour going through my closet before finally settling on a vintage floral dress and a leather jacket. I'd put on some makeup, too. Except for the Halloween party, I hadn't done that since the day Jim had brought me home. Now I was wearing the kind of face that my agent had always insisted on. The one that meant I'd always be camera ready, like I was born with perfect skin and rosy lips. I felt strange, almost as if I were stepping back in time. The last time I'd put that much effort into getting dressed had been back when I was still auditioning. Realizing that gave me a twinge of depression. So much for that solid feeling. But Rob said that was normal, that even a conversion experience didn't mean I wouldn't feel shaky sometimes. It just meant that I could deal with things a little better. Like coming to terms with the past. Like acting. Even if I wasn't ready to return to it yet, it made me feel good to know that one day I would. I was glad I had run into Mrs. Jenkins. Maybe Yale was a distant dream, but it was nice to have it tucked away in a corner of my mind. I held my chin up, something I'd forgotten how to do over the past year, and imagined Claudia in front of me. "What? Oh, no, I don't think I'm coming back to class, Claudia. I've just been waitlisted at Yale." My voice quavered a little at the end. Not the most believable delivery. At least I'd managed to get the words out without bursting into tears. I knew I wouldn't have been able to do that even a month ago.

"Hey, are you okay? I mean, talking to yourself isn't your usual style."

"Dahlia!" I hadn't noticed her waiting by my locker.

"I mean it, are you all right? You looked like you were zoning out again." She seemed worried. She was trying to be her usual sarcastic self, but I could see what she was thinking. After all, it had been only a couple of days ago when I'd treated her to a special showing of my five-year-old voice losing it. But that had been a command performance. I'd retired that act now. Even if the new grounded feeling I had was a little rockier than I'd like, I knew the really bad stuff was behind me. All the nightmare experiences of the past year seemed slightly faded now. As if they were stills from a movie that had been left out in the sun.

"I'm fine, I was just . . . Well, never mind. What's up?"

She studied me closely for a second. I must have looked okay, though, because she seemed relieved. "I got a letter from Daryll this morning. He says he really misses me. He wants us to get back together."

"And?"

"Well, I'm glad he finally came crawling, but I don't know. I mean, I still love him, but maybe my mother's right. Maybe we shouldn't be so serious. I'm only seventeen, you know? I still want to see him, but I think we should cool it for a while."

"Like I keep telling you, I don't know about these things, but it sounds like that's the right thing to do." I could tell that the weekend had had its effect on Dahlia too. She seemed more serious now. Not like she still wouldn't come up with crazy schemes or anything, but like she might think them through for a second first.

"Yeah, well, I hope so. Hey, what do you mean you don't know about these things, you're the one who's fixed up for tonight!"

I blushed. "But this is my first time! Believe me, I don't even know how to act or anything!" We were walking toward the school entrance. "Don't embarrass me when he shows up, okay?"

Dahlia rolled her eyes. "Don't you think I have a little more class than that?" She nudged me in the ribs. "Hey, he's cute! I never really looked at him before." She nodded toward Tim.

"Dahlia!" I hissed between my teeth. But she was right, he did look really cute, even if he wasn't dressed like Heathcliff today. Tim was wearing jeans and a plaid shirt, kind of like a young Jimmy Stewart. I'd forgotten how much I liked Jimmy Stewart.

"Hey, Stephanie. Hi, Dahlia." Tim grinned at us.

"So, I guess I'll give you a call later, Stephanie." Dahlia winked at me, and sashayed off.

"Hi," I said. Then I stopped. Should I ask him how his day had been? No, that sounded too boring. Should I talk about the weather? Definitely not. That was a topic that could wait until we'd been married for thirty years and didn't have anything left to say to each other. The expression on Tim's face embarrassed me a little, and I ducked my head, avoiding his eyes. I felt a little bit awkward, as if it weren't just a date I was going on, but a new chapter of my life that was about to unfold. I felt young and nervous, but also hopeful. I stood holding my books somewhat stiffly. This wasn't something I knew how to do. I'd had experiences that most people twice my age would never know, but this was new to me. I thought back over all the commercials I'd ever auditioned for; surely I must have played the excited teen on a date before. But nothing came to mind. I was on my own. I smiled at Tim a little hesitantly.

But if Tim noticed my shyness, he didn't seem to mind. He put his hand on my arm, his hand resting lightly above my burn scar, and led us both out of the school and into the brilliant sunshine.

DATE DUE